BAREFOOT SUMMER

AND OTHER STORIES

by

Michael Tod

First published in Great Britain by Cadno Books in 2013

cadnobooks@btinternt.com

Michael Tod has asserted his right to be
identified as the author of this book.

www.michaeltod.co.uk

michaeltod@btinternet.com

Cover illustration by Mick Loates

www.mickloates.co.uk

Photo of author by Alan John

ISBN 978-0-95723-0-9

Other books by Michael Tod.

The Silver Tide

The Second Wave

The Golden Flight

Now available as a single volume –

The Dorset Squirrels

Dolphin Song

God's Elephants

A Curlew's Cry (Poetry)

About the Author.

Novelist, poet and philosopher Michael Tod was born in Dorset in 1937. He lived near Weymouth until his family moved to a hill farm in Wales when he was eleven. His childhood experiences on the Dorset coast and in the Welsh mountains gave him a deep love and a knowledge of wild creatures and wild places, which is reflected in his poetry, novels and short stories

Married with three children, three grandchildren and two great grandsons, he still lives, works and walks in his beloved Welsh Hills where Barefoot Summer has its setting.

Contents

BAREFOOT SUMMER

CHAPTER ONE

I love the story of the elderly aristocratic gentleman who would lie in bed in the morning until his butler brought up a newly-ironed copy of that day's *Times* newspaper, opened at the obituaries page. The old gentleman would read the page and, if his name was *not* printed there, he would get out of bed.

I don't recall exactly when the obituaries in *The Daily Telegraph* became compulsory reading for me, probably four or five years ago when I was about seventy. Now I read them even before the news and comment pages, which I suppose is a bit sad. Increasingly I read about people I have known – senior R.A.F. officers I have served under, bishops who I met when they were still parish priests and authors who had been published by the same company that published my work many years ago.

Yesterday I read the obituary for 'Tigerface' Townsend with great interest and sorrow, although I had met him only once and that was half a century ago, back in the early 1960s, but what he told me then has stayed clear in my memory ever since.

The obituary told of his birth in a rundown part of Birmingham, his disfiguring car crash when he was a teenager and how he became one of the BBC's top wildlife photographers. But no mention of the events he related to me on that flight from Nairobi all those years ago and, unusually, there was no reference to him having been married or not, which was what I really wanted to know. But, now that he is dead, I feel that I can reveal the amazing and rather beautiful story of his time in the Welsh mountains that he lovingly described to me as his 'Barefoot Summer'.

Tigerface and I met on a Royal Air Force trooping plane at Nairobi's Embakasi Airport in May 1962. I was on my way home for demobilisation from the R.A.F. and he was a fellow passenger, even though he had never been in the services. I don't know how he fixed the flight but civilian flights were horrifically expensive then and, in those days, things like that could be fixed if you knew who to speak with. I expect it is very different now.

The pilot of the aircraft, a Bristol Britannia, known in the popular press at the time as the Whispering Giant, was Flight Lieutenant (Chalky) White, who had been an apprentice at R.A.F. Halton at the same time as I had been there, before he had been selected for aircrew training. I had met him again the evening before that flight in the mess at R.A.F Eastleigh and, after a drink or two, I had persuaded him to make a slight detour from the official route to fly past Mount Kenya, which I had climbed a few months before. Mount Kenya, like its sister mountain to the south, Kilimanjaro, is an extinct volcano and is known to the locals as Kerinyaga. Several local tribes believe that it is where their gods live. It must be one of the most beautiful mountains in the world and I can see why they would believe that. It was unlikely that I would ever come back to East Africa after my demob and I just wanted another look.

There were plenty of empty seats on the plane but a man with a badly scarred face indicated that he would like to sit next to me and I was quite happy about that. I was intrigued by the shiny scars disfiguring both sides of his face, which looked like the stripes on the face of a tiger. Such flights were long and boring and company is often welcome. I didn't know at that time he was not a fellow serviceman as, for some strange political reason, all servicemen and women on transit flights wore civilian clothes and our passports described us as Government Officials.

I half rose, held out my hand and said 'Michael – Michael Tod.' He took my hand, shook it and said, 'David, but everyone calls me Tigerface – Tigerface Townsend'.

Earlier in my service career, I had met a few ex-aircrew who had similar disfigurements from aircraft crashes during the war but such veterans had virtually all retired by that time. This man obviously sensed my curiosity and offered an explanation. 'My face? In a car crash as a boy. Stupid, nasty business – two of my mates killed and me, who was driving, left looking like this. Got used to it now. I hope it doesn't bother you.'

'Not at all,' I replied, glad it was out in the open. 'Seen a few like that in my time. I thought it must be from a prang.'

'I haven't been in the services. I'm a photographer – wildlife – animals, birds and the like.' He looked round, a touch guiltily, to see if he was being overheard. 'Shouldn't really be on this flight but a friend fixed it. I missed my proper flight a week ago when I got stuck up-country.'

'Your secret's safe with me,' I said and then told him how I hoped that the pilot would fly close to Mount Kenya after an unofficial request from me. He grinned and I felt that our individual rule-bending had created a bond between us.

'I've been working up-country north of there,' he told me. 'Filming warthogs mostly. I got some good footage – especially of one being chased by a lioness. She nearly caught the piggy but it reached its burrow just in time, spun round and backed into it. The lioness took one look down the hole, saw the tusks facing her and walked away, trying to look as if she hadn't really wanted to catch it anyway. Did you say we were going to fly past the mountain?'

'The pilot promised to – but if we don't take off soon it'll be too late.' I glanced at my watch. 'Still time to see the peaks in the sunset if we get away shortly.'

Doors were being closed and engines run up. After a few minutes, the airport buildings started to move past the windows and soon we were in position for take-off. I had chosen a starboard window seat for the best view of the mountain if Chalky was able to deliver the goods.

The timing was perfect. We flew past the peaks at a similar altitude to the summit, the mists which normally hide the mountain in the daytime had lifted and we were looking directly out at the glaciers, now glowing pink from the setting sun and with the shadows of the gullies a deep purple. I imagined the elephants and the surly buffalo in the forests below and said a mental goodbye to the country I had come to love.

All too soon, it was all out of sight behind us and hot drinks were being brought round as the equatorial night closed in.

Tigerface and I made small talk over the coffee until I asked him about filming animals, when he really became animated. I learned a lot from him in the next half hour. But what he told me put paid to my long-held secret ambition that I would try and find a job as a wildlife film-maker after my coming demob. I had dabbled with 8mm cameras and films since I was a boy and rather fancied I was good at it. What I learned from Tigerface made me realise that it wasn't for me. Most of his time on location was spent sitting silently in a hide for hours, or even days at a time waiting for something to happen. Often nothing does.

I knew *I* couldn't take that. My whole life has been based on action and making things happen by *doing something*, so I knew that such a career was not for me.

I kept quiet while my ambitions in that direction flew out of the window but I was still interested in what he was telling me, and I asked him how many people made up a film-crew in the bush.

'In Africa there are usually a dozen or so. Besides the camera-men and sound-recording staff – usually all white men – there are drivers, cooks and porters–mostly locals. I don't operate like that. On this trip there was just my assistant, Daniel M'wangi, and me in a Land Rover. We would set up camp together and he would cook the evening meal whilst I checked and cleaned the cameras and reloaded the film if we had used any during that day. Daniel M'wangi spoke very good English. His father had been a Christian missionary from England and his mother a native girl. Probably he was the result of an illicit relationship but he was great guy and became a close friend.'

'Was he a Christian?' I asked.

'Difficult to tell! He liked to be called by the biblical name his father had given him as well as the native one from his mother. We often discussed religious things over the campfire before turning in. He spoke with great respect for the teachings from the bible which his missionary father had instilled in him but he believed, like most of the people in his tribe, that God lived on the top of Mount Kenya and that Jesus was probably up there too.'

Rather facetiously, I made some remark about not meeting either of them when I had been on the mountain recently and that I'd probably missed them both because I had stayed lower down with altitude sickness.

Tigerface ignored my remark, which was a relief as I had regretted it immediately, and he asked about my climb. He seemed genuinely interested as I described the giant groundsel plants, the lofty lobelias and the heather that grew up to ten feet high. When I described the rock hyraxes that lived among the boulders at high altitude, he asked a lot of questions about those. I didn't know much, other than that they were supposed to be first cousins to elephants. He must have been intrigued because, many years later, I saw a BBC Natural World film about them on television, with Tigerface's name leading the credits.

By the time the blankets and pillows were being issued and the cabin lights were being turned down, I felt that I had known him all my life.

CHAPTER TWO

Tigerface and I pressed the buttons to make the seats tilt back as far as they would go and tried to sleep. It seemed that, like me, he wasn't ready and, as there were no occupied seats near us, we started to talk again, keeping our voices low. I was still thinking about wildlife photography and asked him how he got started in that business.

'It's a long story,' he said.

'We've got all night,' I replied, but not expecting it to take that long.

'I told you about the car crash which caused this.' He made a movement with his hand towards his face in the semi-darkness. 'If that hadn't happened, I'd probably be driving a forklift truck in a Birmingham warehouse now.'

We tilted our seats forward again so as to be able to speak more easily and I waited for him to continue. He seemed to be organising his thoughts or perhaps deciding how much of his early life he was going to reveal to someone who had been a complete stranger just an hour or two before.

'I was born in Birmingham a couple of years before the war – 1937. My father was called up in 1940 and went into the Royal Artillery. My mother had trained as a nurse before she got married but had given that up when I came along. I was eight before my father came out of the army and got a job driving a taxi, which he did for the rest of his life. At first we lived in a Prefab which I rather liked but, when these were demolished, we were given a council flat in a tower block, which I hated. I failed my eleven plus. I didn't try much because, if I passed, I knew I would go to a different school to all my mates. Knowing what happened later, it would have been better if I had.'

He paused and I said, 'The car crash?'

'Yes,' he replied. 'I got in with a bad bunch – not a gang as such – but a group who smoked, drank when we could get some, and would nick any cars we could find unlocked and drive them about. We weren't evil – just bored. One night when I was fifteen, three of us found a car, my mate Bill, hotwired it – he was an expert at that – and we went for a drive. Nowhere in particular. I was driving and Billy looked out of the back window and told me we were being followed. When the blue light started flashing, I panicked and put my foot down hard. I never found out what we hit but I went through the windscreen and Billy and Winston were killed. I came round in a hospital ward, bandages all around my head with just slots for my eyes, nose and mouth. My mother and father were sitting by the bed, Mum crying and Dad looking stern. It was weeks before they told me about Bill and Winston, though I had worked out that they were dead when I realised that neither of them came to see me – and that nobody mentioned their names.'

Tigerface paused again and I felt it was my turn to say something. 'Nasty business.' I said, and it sounded weak and inadequate.

'It was!' Tigerface replied and went on. 'I won't bore you with all the medical details but I was in hospital for months and it was a long time before anyone would let me near a mirror. When I did get home, I wouldn't go out. I didn't want people staring at me or whispering that I was the one who had killed their sons or brothers.'

He paused again and asked, 'Are you sure you want to hear all this?'

I assured him that I did and he went on. 'It was early May and there must have been some kind of family discussion I was left out of and it was decided that I would go and spend the summer with a woman who had been a nurse with Mum back before I was born. She lived on a farm – or so we thought – in a wild part of Wales.

'Mum called her Becca but she had always been Aunt Becca to me. As far back as I could remember I had always had a present in the post from her at Christmas and for my birthdays – usually a hand-knitted jumper or a woolly hat and I had to write a thank-you letter. When I was old enough to write the address, I was puzzled by the name of the farm. I would write *Talybwlch Farm* and think – what a funny name. Now I know the word is Welsh for 'at the foot of the pass'.

Chalky White, the pilot, walked down the aisle doing the rounds, having left the co-pilot at the controls.

He saw I was awake and stopped to ask if I was OK. I introduced Tigerface to him, naming him as 'David Townsend.'

'Oh yes. Hello.' Chalky looked around furtively and, when he could see no one else was listening, he continued, 'You'll be the film-making man?'

'That's me. Thanks if you had anything to do with me being...'

'Don't mention it. Even with the crew's private crates of pineapples in the hold, we're well under capacity. Maybe you can do me a favour sometime.'

' If I can, I ...' Tigerface started to say, but Chalky had moved on down the aisle, his head turning from side to side to ensure that everything was as it should be.

When he had gone Tigerface asked, 'Where was I? Or have you had enough? Would you like to sleep now?' He was obviously afraid that he might be boring me but nothing was further from the truth, so I replied, 'No – I'm fascinated – please tell me more.'

He wriggled into a more comfortable position.

'Mum had never been to the farm and I'd created a picture in my mind of a white-washed low farmhouse surrounded by green fields full of cows and sheep and, because it was in Wales, I had pictured stark mountains in the background where red-coloured dragons lived. The dragons had flown away by the time I was seven but the rest of the picture was still vivid in my mind.'

I smiled at the idea of the dragons flying away because he didn't believe in them any more.

One of the crew interrupted us politely, offering to bring Horlicks – or it might have been Ovaltine. They had probably been told by Chalky that two passengers were still awake. We both refused and I suggested coffees, as I knew they would keep us awake and I wanted to hear more of Tigerface's story.

'My dad was not keen on my going. I had overheard a row about it. Dad was saying, "I don't want him down there in bloody Wales with that nutty friend of yours!" and Mum was saying that Becca was not nutty, just a bit different, and she would look after me well. Then she went on to say that Becca was an ideal person as she was a qualified nurse and had worked with Archie McIndoe in the war.'

I knew Archie McIndoe as the surgeon who had rebuilt many airmens' burnt and smashed up faces and I could see that Tigerface's mother had a point.

'Mum said, "I can't take any more time off work to look after David. We need the money – you know we're behind with the rent already." I felt bad then as it was all my fault so, when they suggested the idea to me, I feigned eagerness, although I just wanted to stay in the flat away from other people. So Mum wrote to Aunt Becca and she wrote back at once, saying that she would love to have me there for the summer. Dad was driving a taxi at that time and he must have got permission to have it for himself for a day because he drove me down to Wales. Mum wanted to come but she couldn't get the day off work.

'Remember in those days – it was 1953 – Coronation Year –not many ordinary people had cars and televisions were rare. *We* didn't have one. Schools, like the one I went to, didn't do outings and I don't think I'd ever been out of Brum. It seems far-fetched to say that I saw my first real cows and sheep that day, when I was fifteen but I am sure that it's true. If I hadn't been feeling so bad about leaving Mum, and all the trouble I'd caused by my stupidity, I would have been really excited and happy. Just as we were leaving, she gave me a shiny, newly-minted Crown piece, which I briefly thanked her for and slipped it into my back trousers' pocket to keep it separate from the few ordinary coins in the side pockets. I think now that she had meant it as a kind of talisman to keep me safe while I was away.

'Being a taxi-driver, Dad knew the way around Brum like the back of his hand but, once we reached Wales, he had to use a map to find the village nearest to Aunt Becca's which was called Groesvaen. When we got there, he asked a man the way to Talybwlch Farm and had to repeat the name three times before the man understood what Dad was asking. It was then about midday – we had made an early start because Dad had to get the taxi back that night.

'The last part of the road up to the farm was just two cracked and broken concrete strips and Dad was concerned about the springs. And, when we got to the end of the track – one could hardly call it a road – it wasn't the low white-washed farm house that I had always pictured but a run-down and deserted army camp. There were rows of huts just like the ones in a film I had recently seen – about prisoners of war in Germany – called *The Wooden Horse*. But these huts were set among bushes, and the fence around them was covered in ivy and creepers. Goats and chickens wandered between the huts and, if it wasn't that Aunt Becca was standing outside the only permanent looking building, I know we would have thought we had taken a wrong road. The solidly defiant building I recognised as having been the camp guardroom by its flat overhanging veranda and the low concrete platform on which it stood. Such buildings had often appeared in Newsreel films I had seen.

'Dad got stiffly out of the driving seat and went over to her while I stayed in the taxi hiding my face. I hated meeting new people, looking as I did. Aunt Becca came around the taxi, opened the door, looked me straight in the face without a flicker of surprise or distaste, helped me out and gave me a warm hug. I couldn't remember even my Mum giving me a hug as warm as that one – we didn't go in for that sort of thing much at home. I loved her from that moment on.

'We all stepped up onto the concrete apron around the old guardroom and went inside. There was a wood-burning stove with chopped planks stacked near by.

These looked like bits of one of the wooden huts and later, when I had chopped up some of these myself, I learned that this was just what they were. Next to it was a free-standing oven, topped with two gas burners, behind which was a Calor Gas cylinder. Aunt Becca lit the gas and boiled a kettle whilst she answered Dad's questions about where the farm had gone.

'Before the war, it was right here,' she told him. 'Then the army came and requisitioned it, and the valley behind, for a gunnery range. They knocked down all the farm building and put these things up!' There was resentment – almost savagery – in her voice. 'I was away in England, nursing burnt airmen, and the Army just gave my parents five days to pack up the house, dispose of the animals and move down into the village to live. They were given a small amount of money as compensation but they were heart-broken and my Da had died even before my next leave and Mam followed soon after.'

Tigerface stopped and I could see he was still emotionally involved, even some ten or eleven years on. After a brief pause, he continued. 'I could see that Dad wanted to get back to Birmingham before it got dark and he was eager to get away – but reluctant to leave me there. I rather liked the *shenzi* feel of the place and wanted to stay.'

Tigerface must have picked up the word *shenzi* whilst he'd been in Kenya. It's a Swahili word meaning

23

rundown and tatty – I still use it myself as there is no English word that means exactly the same thing – think of the sheds on well-established allotments! How would you define those with one word? *Shenzi* fits perfectly!

'Dad insisted on seeing where I would sleep – which was in one of three prisoners' cells at the back of the Guardroom. Aunt Becca slept in one of the other cells and the third was a storeroom. There was also a proper toilet but in front of the seat was an Elsan bucket.

'The bloody men from the Ministry cut off the water when I moved in here,' she told me. 'I wanted my farm back but they said it was not allowed under some stupid regulations. I stayed here anyway and they've been trying to get rid of me ever since. I'm not going though - whatever they do!'

'I could see Dad was trying to find a way for me not to stay. "What do you do for a water supply then?" he asked.

"I fetch water for the stock from the stream and drinking water for me from a spring up the hill. It's quite pure – my family have been drinking that water for centuries."

'If Dad had been on his own I know that he'd have been off home in a flash but I made it clear that I was going to stay and he was persuaded to drink a mug of tea before he wished me an awkward goodbye and drove off down the track as though my childhood dragons were after him.'

Tigerface chuckled at the memory and I said, 'Probably did the taxi's springs a lot of no good!'

CHAPTER THREE

The advertising man who had invented the phrase 'The Whispering Giant' for the Britannia aircraft was living up to the reputation of his profession. Compared with modern jets they were really quite noisy and the engines roared and droned as the four huge propellers hauled the plane and its passengers across Sudan and the wastes of the Sahara Desert some twenty-four thousand feet below.

Tigerface excused himself and went aft to the toilet and, when he returned, I did the same.

'Still interested in my story?' he asked as I sat down again next to him. I assured him I was, even though I did want to sleep.

He pulled the issue blanket around his knees and said, 'Aunt Becca was not very tall, she had dark hair and a complexion which came from being out of doors much of the time. Her eyes were a honey colour and were warm and bright and glowed in a way which sort of implied that she knew something no one else did. I loved her immediately and I am sure that she felt the same way about me despite my looks, which were quite hideous at that time.

'I learned from Mum later that she had been engaged during the war to one of the injured pilots she had been nursing but, when he was fit to fly again, he was shot down on a raid over Germany. Perhaps she saw me as the son she was never going to have.

'We had lunch after Dad had left – boiled egg and goats-milk-cheese sandwiches, which we ate sitting on a plank bench under the projecting concrete balcony of the guardroom which was so obviously *home* to her. Then she showed me around what was left of the Army Camp. There had once been about twenty of the wooden huts but she had been demolishing them one by one for firewood and for timber to make fences. There were now about sixteen left intact – some were empty and some housed goats or chickens. One had been a workshop and many of the tools had been left behind when the camp was abandoned, together with work-benches fitted with a variety of vices. The locks on all the huts had been forced but I didn't ask who had done that.

'Some huts had army-style metal beds – you know the sort – with tubular frames and bases made with wire in diamond patterns. Quite a lot of these she had taken outside over the years and wired together on edge to make pens for the goats. One other hut in the middle of the camp had toilet bowls, all empty, a three bay urinal, wash-basins and two baths – but none of the taps were working.

'Then she took me way up the hill to the fresh-water spring to fetch drinking water. Here she showed me where the officials, who she said, 'wanted her out,' had turned off the supply that fed the pipes to the camp and put a big padlock on the wheel which opened and closed the valve.

'Later that day I took a rusty hack-saw from the workshop hut and sawed through the padlock and, with a big spanner, managed to get the water running down to the camp and into the taps and the toilets. I'd never had much respect for authority and had no qualms about what I was doing. Aunt Becca's face when she heard the toilet cistern filling was a joy and she kissed my ugly forehead and called me 'her darling boy'!

'I spent the next few days exploring the camp and the fields up as far as the fence which separated them from the mountain and heath-land and doing little jobs for Aunt Becca around the camp.'

I must have yawned then as Tigerface stopped and said, 'We should try and get some sleep – there'll be plenty of time tomorrow if you want to hear more.'

I said that I 'would look forward to that', pulled the blanket up around my shoulders and eventually slept, my dreams full of goats, chickens and toilet bowls filling for the first time in years.

When I woke, Tigerface was not in the seat next to me but returned shortly, freshly shaved and eager for one of the breakfasts that were being brought round on little trays. It was light outside and far below, through the window, I could see sand dunes but nothing else. After the breakfast trays had been taken away, I washed and shaved, then settled back in my seat to hear the rest of Tigerface's story.

'There was something I forgot to tell you last night,' he said. 'In the Guard Room where we were living was a loom on which Aunt Becca wove things like blankets and scarves. Before I went to bed on the first night, she gave me a blanket which she said she had made for me when she knew I was coming there. It was big enough to cover a single bed comfortably and on the one side was a picture of a castle in bright sunlight and on the other side was the same scene – but covered in snow. Being ignorant about weaving and textiles then I never even thought how it could have been made like that but just accepted it as a gift for making the water run again.

'What was really special about the blanket was that, if I got under it sunny-side up when the air was cold, I was warm but, if I turned it over when it was hot, it kept me cool. It seemed like magic then – and it still does now when I look back!'

'Have you still got it?' I asked.

'Oh yes. I wouldn't be without it – especially on safari. It's in my luggage in the hold.'

I wanted to see this 'magic' blanket but thought it unlikely that I ever would.

'I'll show it to you if I get a chance,' Tigerface said and continued with his story. 'The first few days and nights there were quite cool and I slept in the little prisoner's cell with the blanket over me, sunny-side up and was snug and warm. There was another special thing about the blanket that I didn't realise at the time. When I used it, the air around smelt faintly of honeysuckle although I didn't recognise the scent then, never having seen honeysuckle before I came down to Wales.

After a few days the weather changed and one night I was so hot in the cell with its tiny window, that Aunt Becca helped me take my bed to pieces and carry it out onto the veranda of the guardroom. We set it up with the blanket snowy-side up and I undressed and got into my bed there. Sure enough, I was comfortably cool and lay there, looking at the stars beyond the veranda roof and marvelling at how many there were, especially after Aunt Becca turned out the paraffin lantern inside.

'I must have slept for only a little while before I woke up, needing a pee. I didn't want to wake Aunt Becca so I got out of bed and, barefoot, tiptoed to the edge of the concrete, stood there and started to pee into the darkness. Somewhere among the dark huts I could hear someone playing Lilli Marlene on a mouth organ. Then I heard a voice from the same direction shout, "Put that bloody light out!"

'Standing there barefoot in the darkness, I could hear other muffled voices – it seemed that the camp was alive again – and I was peeing on my foot!'

Tigerface smiled at the memory and I began to understand that this was no ordinary childhood memory that he was relating.

'Strangely I wasn't scared – just intrigued. The voices weren't hostile – quite the opposite. I felt that I was meant to be there – that I was one of them – one of the soldiers who was far from home and using this mountain and Aunt Becca's farm to learn how to kill other soldiers. I went back to the bed, dried my foot with a corner of the blanket and got into bed again.

'As soon as my feet were off the ground the music and the voices stopped as though someone had turned off a switch. I lay there for a minute or two, then sat up and put my feet back on the concrete slab. Once more I could hear voices but now the mouth organ was playing "There'll be bluebirds over…" – you know the one.'

I did. It had always been a favourite of mine, especially when it was sung by Vera Lynn, even though I knew that bluebirds didn't fly over those cliffs, unless you called swallows, "blue birds".

The tune came into my head and I hummed a few bars to myself. Tigerface was saying, 'Feet on the ground – voices and music. Feet off the ground – silence, except for noises from the goats' pen and an owl calling far away. I did it a dozen times, then pulled the blanket up and slept.'

'You weren't scared?' I asked. 'I'd have been!'

'It wasn't scary at all. It was as if all the voices were of mates and I even knew the soldier playing the mouth organ was called "Jack".'

'Did you tell your Aunt Becca?' I asked.

'Yes – in the morning. She just asked if it worried me and, when I said "No," she said, "That's alright then," and neither of us mentioned it again. I often slept outside after that and it was always the same.

'Once a week, on market days, the wife of a neighbour drove up to the farm in a Land Rover and took Aunt Becca down to the nearest town, which was called Abergavenny, to shop.'

I knew Abergavenny. I had camped near there when I was in the Scouts and, to the west and north of it were the Brecon Beacons and the Black Mountains. Having hiked through that area then I had some idea of where Tigerface has been staying but kept quiet so as not to interrupt his story.

'Of course, each week she asked me to come with her but I always refused, conscious of my looks, and I rather enjoyed having the place to myself.

'After about the third time, when I was well settled in and the day was hot, I waited until the Land Rover was out of sight and walked a mile or so up through the fields beside the stream. I climbed over a stone stile and was on the open mountain at the foot of a wide valley that I later learned the Welsh call a *cwm*. The vegetation was mostly rough grass and bracken with a few scattered hawthorn trees and I could hear curlews calling but didn't know what they were then. As I wandered on a dipper was flying up the stream, landing around each bend out of my sight and then flying up again as I got near. Two buzzards circled above me, mewing like cats and the whole scene was magical and exciting to me. Even the grazing sheep seemed special. Remember I was a city boy who had never been anywhere like this before. As I said before – magical!

'Round a bend further upstream, I saw a huge lump of grey metal in the stream-bed. I recognised it as an aero-engine from the books I had read and from the films I had seen and wondered how it had got there. I soon found out!

'Naturally, as boys do, I wanted to touch it and fiddle with the various bits projecting from it. I sat on a stone, took off my shoes and socks, rolled up my trouser legs and waded into the water, which was surprisingly warm and came to just below my knees. My feet were quite tender then – they got much tougher later – and I was concentrating on where I was stepping. As soon as I touched the engine, I was drawn into another scene! There was a roaring in my ears, everything had gone black and a voice with an American accent was shouting, "Where in the hell are we, Mac?"

'Then there was an almighty flash and a bang and I was lying on my back in the water, soaked to the skin and hurting all over. I got to my feet and waded to the shore. The aero engine was still in the bed of the stream, looking just as it had before, so I sat quietly watching it, then put my shoes and socks on to my wet feet and almost ran back down to the camp. I knew Aunt Becca would not be home for hours so I hung my wet clothes up to dry on the line between two huts as Aunt Becca always did, and mooched about the camp until she came back.

'Later, I asked her about the engine. "Oh, you found that then," she replied, apparently unconcerned about me wandering off on my own. "Nasty, sad business that. An American plane, I think they called it a Dakota, flew into the mountain in the dark – just before the end of the war. All the crew were killed and soldiers from the camp carried the bodies down. The rest of the plane and its other engine are still up on the mountain. The one engine must have rolled down into the stream – I've seen it there myself."

'Just a day before that, if someone had told me where to find a crashed plane – like any boy I'd have been there like a shot. But not after what had happened to me! I didn't tell Aunt Becca about my experience of being in the crash. I didn't think she would believe me.'

I thought that Tigerface was looking a bit shaken. It was obvious that the incident was still strong in his mind even after some ten or eleven years, so I asked a question to take his mind away from it for a while. 'What did you live on?'

'Mostly eggs and cheese that Aunt Becca made from the goats' milk, and veggies which she grew in a plot behind the guardroom. She would buy porridge oats, bread and fruit when she went to Abergavenny and she would sell eggs and cheeses in the market there. Sometimes, for a treat, she would kill and pluck a chicken and later on, she would gather wild mushrooms, which she would cook in butter and milk.'

'Did she keep any sheep?' I asked.

'There were sheep all around in the fields and on the mountain but I think they belonged to a neighbour. She had nothing to do with them unless they got through our fence and into the veggie patch.'

I was building up a vivid picture of the place in my mind and rather wanted to be there. I was even envying Tigerface his time in Wales. At that age I'd been in school, resenting being indoors, especially when it was sunny.

'What did you and your aunt do in the days?' I asked.

'There were plenty of things to be done – but no hurry to do any of them. We often worked together, collecting the eggs and planting seeds in the veggie plot. I learned how to milk the goats and make cheese and I would muck out the huts where the goats and the chickens lived. I'd barrow the muck round and spread it where the veggies were to grow. For a city boy it was all new and exciting and I'd virtually forgotten my face – which was healing well. Aunt Becca would examine the scars every few days with her 'nurses' expression on her face and say, "Coming along nicely, those'.

'There was a heat-wave that spring. I had brought few clothes with me – a duffle coat, a couple of vests, three shirts, some socks, two pairs of pyjamas and two pairs of long trousers – most boys of my class didn't wear underpants in those days. One day, after I'd been carting goat muck and was sweating from the heat and the effort and we were sitting drinking tea in the shade, Aunt Becca asked if I had any shorts. I did have a pair of soccer shorts but they were at home in Birmingham so I shook my head and said that I should have brought those but no one had thought I would be playing soccer on a Welsh mountain.

"Come over by here," she said and reached for a pair of scissors from a basket by her chair. I stood in front of her and she poked the end of the scissors through the fabric of my trousers and cut the legs off a few inches above my knees. I shook the cut-off legs down to my feet and stepped out of them.

"Take those off and I'll hem up the cut edges," she said which left me in a bit of a quandary. My other pair had just been washed and were hanging on the line outside to dry.

'I'll put my pyjama trousers on,' I said and she laughed.

"For God's sake. I was a nurse for years. Do you think I don't know what a man looks like?"

I was unsure what to do. I hadn't even let Mum see me since I was about twelve and starting to grow hair down there. But I was flattered to have been considered, even obliquely, as a man. So I took them off and handed them over, wishing my shirt tails were a bit longer. Aunt Becca glanced at me and smiled. "Nothing to be ashamed of there!" she said and I was curiously happy.

'Aunt Becca got a black Singer sewing-machine out of a cupboard and in a couple of minutes had turned the cut-edges in and with me, still half-naked, cranking the handle, she stitched a tidy hem on each leg. I put my new shorts on with a mixture of relief and regret. Looking back now, I realise that this was the first stirrings of real sexual awareness. Boys, and I suppose girls too, were much more innocent then. I went to an all-boys school, I didn't have any sisters and there was no television in most houses – certainly not in ours. Our parents were far too embarrassed to discuss such things with their children and there weren't any easy words to use anyway. The words other children used were considered 'dirty' and medical terms were largely unknown in my class of people then.'

Tigerface seemed to have forgotten that I was of a similar age to him but, as I had suffered from the same stupid ignorance, I could identify with his feelings absolutely. I once again wondered why he was telling me all this but he had certainly caught my attention. He was about to continue when the sound of the aircraft engines altered and the captain's voice announced that we would shortly be landing at Tripoli to refuel. It was hard to come away from that 'magical' Welsh hillside but we clicked our seats fully upright, fastened our seat belts and sat in silence as the pilot brought the 'Whispering Giant' down onto the desert runway.

As we went down the steps from the aircraft, the glare of the sun hurt our eyes and waves of heat washed around us even though it was quite early in the morning. The reception area was just a few corrugated iron buildings, each as hot as an oven and we hoped to be on our way before long. Tigerface and I sat at a metal table sipping luke-warm beer and watching the other passengers. Some of the servicemen's families had small children with them who were obviously hot and uncomfortable but the female crew members were helping with these. I was looking forward to getting back on board and hearing the rest of Tigerface's story but, after an hour or so Chalky White, the pilot, came round to each table and apologised for the fact that there was to be a delay due to 'a small technical problem'. Had I been on my own I would have asked what it was but there was a kind of convention amongst airmen that civilians were not to know too much, so I just thanked him and said something fairly meaningless like, 'Not too long, I hope!'

Tigerface ordered two more beers from the wandering waiter and suggested that, if I liked, he would tell me more about his 'Barefoot Summer'.

'That sounds like the title of a book,' I said and he replied, 'No one would believe the story if I wrote it down. But it did happen!'

I replied, 'Try it on me.'

I took my beer from the tray held by the waiter in the long white robe, asking if he would take East African

Shillings as payment. He would and did and was happy to keep the change from the two notes I gave him.

Tigerface sipped his beer and seemed to be trying to remember where he had got too.

'Your Aunt had just cut the legs off your trousers,' I prompted him and he said, 'Ah yes. I hadn't worn shorts, other than for games, since I went to secondary school and I'd forgotten what freedom they gave.'

For the last two and a half years in Nairobi, I had worn shorts every day and was not looking forward to switching back to the uniform we wore at home. *Home* being the U.K. if you were a Brit living or working abroad. I knew just what he meant.

Tigerface pushed his chair back and continued his story. 'It was still very hot in that part of Wales and I thought I would go back up the mountain. I had no intention of touching or even going near that engine again, but I thought I would explore further up the valley. I asked Aunt Becca if it was O.K. and she agreed quite readily. There was just a hint of a breeze when I climbed over the stile between the fields and the mountain. I was wearing my new shorts and I took my shirt off and tied it round my waist by the sleeves. I could hear the curlews again and sheep ran away from me into the bracken as I followed a path of soft green grass that led up the valley parallel to the stream and about a hundred yards away from it.

'Quite a long way above the place where the engine was, the stream and the path converged at a little stone bridge at the lower end of a big pool of water and I saw a dipper fly across the pool and disappear where there was a rock outcrop at the top end of the pool. Trees, which I later learned were birches and mountain ashes, grew out of the cracks in the rocks and I suspected that the dipper had a nest there so I walked around the pool, over grass as smooth as the bowling green in the park near where I lived, until I was opposite where the bird had gone. It flew out just as I got there and I was sure that there must be nest in the rocks. Forgetting about what had happened to me before when I was barefoot, I took off my shoes and socks and waded across the stream, which was shallow there, although the pool into which it ran looked as if it was deep enough to swim in.

'I heard cheeping noises and found a nest with young birds in it in a cavity under an overhanging rock. My foot slipped on a patch of green slime and I grabbed a branch to stop myself falling into the pool. As I swung round, I saw that the whole scene beyond the pool had subtly changed. Where there had been barren hillside there were clumps of trees, delicate birches with silvery bark, groups of elegantly grotesque fir trees and stands of mountain ash covered with creamy-white flowers – and all the sheep had gone!

'I stood under the trees which were growing in the rocks and stared out from the shadows, across the pool, wondering what had happened. Then I saw someone coming down the track towards the bridge. It was a girl of about my own age, dressed in a simple, short-sleeved, green dress which just reached her knees. On her head was a wide-brimmed straw hat – and she, like myself, was barefoot! She was walking quite quickly, as if she wanted to *be* somewhere, if you know what I mean. I didn't know whether to show myself and possibly frighten her or stay hidden until she had gone past. Before I could decide, she turned off the track onto the grassy place by the pool, took off her hat and laid it on the grass beside her, glanced around then, in a movement that would be hard to describe, reached both arms over her shoulders and pulled her dress up and over her head and dropped it on the grass. I was momentarily surprised that she was not wearing any bra or knickers – at that time I thought all big girls and women wore those – but was struck by the grace and elegance of her movements. If I am honest, I fell in love with her at that moment.

'She waded into the pool up to her waist then leaned forward and swam about for a few minutes as I kept hidden under the trees, concerned lest she swim to the top end of the pool and saw me.'

In the heat of the corrugated-iron sheds – they were little more than that – I envied the girl her cooling swim but was eager for Tigerface to continue. Would he show himself or stay hidden?

He answered my unspoken question. 'I decided to stay hidden, not just for fear of scaring her but, to be honest again, I was a teenage boy and one of my fantasies was being acted out before my eyes. I watched her as she waded out of the pool, climbed up the grassy bank and sat in the sun to dry. Then she wriggled into her dress, put her hat on and looked towards where I was hiding. I felt that she *had* seen me but her expression never changed and she turned away and walked quite briskly up the track the way she had come, bare-footed as before.

'When I was quite sure she had gone, I waded back across the stream, sat on the grass, used my shirt to dry my feet and put my socks and shoes on. She had apparently not noticed these. A sheep bleated behind me and, when I raised my head, the clumps of trees were gone and the bare hillside was as it had been before, with just a few hawthorns and a scattering of sheep.

'Something really clicked then and I took off my shoes and socks and stood up. Mysteriously, as in a film, the landscape was changing, the sheep were fading away and the clumps of trees were emerging as if from a mist. Only the pool and the stone bridge were the same. I hoped to see the girl but I knew that she wasn't coming back, that day at least, so I walked down the path, carrying my shoes with my socks rolled up inside them, as far as the stone stile. I sat on the step and put them back on and watched the scene change as it had earlier, but with the trees fading away and the hawthorns and the sheep emerging from a mist.'

Tigerface paused here. 'If you don't believe any of this, I'll stop here and you can write me off as some kind of nutter.'

'No – I'm fascinated. Did you tell your aunt about the girl?'

'I wondered whether I should but it was too personal and too special – and I hoped to see her again the next day.'

'And did you?' I asked.

'Oh, yes. In the morning I did what I regarded by now as my *chores*, ate a sandwich and went off up the valley, going barefoot from the stile up, the path running between the pine trees and the birches that had reappeared as mysteriously as before. I found that the grass of the path felt good under my feet and I was more alert and alive than I had ever felt before. I had hidden my shoes and socks in a clump of bracken near the stile and tied my shirt around my waist as I had the day before and the tiny, wandering breezes were deliciously cool on my bare skin.

'The girl was sitting on the low stone parapet of the bridge as though she was waiting for me, wearing the same green dress and floppy-brimmed hat.

'I approached carefully so as not to alarm her and stopped just before the bridge to give her the opportunity to ignore me or recognise me in some way. I half expected her to fade away, or even run away but, when I got near enough to see that her eyes were an unusual violet colour, she rather shyly said, "What is your name? People call me Bedwen."

"I'm David," I replied and she repeated the name and then said, "I'll call you Dewi." She pronounced it 'Dowey' and I learned later that is the Welsh for David. There was none of the tension that often goes with first meetings – it was as though we had met often before. "I saw you watching me swimming yesterday," she said and although there was no suggestion of an accusation in her tone, I was immediately on the defensive and started to apologise. "I didn't mean to..." I started to say but she laughed. "The soldiers often used to hide and watch me," she said. "But I didn't really mind as long as they didn't try to touch me."

"Soldiers from the camp?" I asked, doing a quick calculation in my head. If she was now fifteen or sixteen, as I thought, she would only have been about eight or nine when the camp was closed. Before I could follow this through, she said, "Yes, and those from the castle."

"Castle?" I asked looking puzzled.

'Up there,' she said, pointing up the track she had come down the day before.

'I stepped up and stood on the parapet of the bridge but there was a low rise in the ground hiding the skyline beyond. "Will I see it if I walk on up there?" As I asked, I wished I had said, "if *we*". I didn't want to lose sight of her!'

"I'll show you," she replied to my relief and we walked up the track, with her keeping about four feet of space between us.

'A hundred yards on, from the top of the rise, I could see a rampart of cliffs at the head of the valley with a gap between them. Right in the gap was the outline of a small castle. All boys love castles and I asked if we could go and look at it.

'Not today,' she said. 'Perhaps tomorrow.'

'This suggested that she was going to be around for a few days at least and I was pleased by that.

'Now we will go back to the pool and I will make you a hat like mine,' she said and there was a degree of authority in her voice. 'It is too hot not to have a hat.'

'I was only too happy to oblige. Keeping the same distance apart, we strolled down to the pool and she started to pick some of the thin green rushes that grew in damp patches nearby. I watched her until she sat down, cross-legged, with the bunch she had picked on the grass beside her, and started to plait some of the rushes together. I stood watching her work for while and could see that she would need more so I picked some myself. I offered her the bunch I'd picked but she wouldn't take them from me – just indicated that I should lay them on the grass where she could reach them. "We must not touch each other," she said simply and, at the time, I did not recognise the importance of what she was saying.

'Why don't you swim in the pool while I make this for you,' she said, without looking up.

'This caught me off guard and I mumbled something stupid about not having brought my bathers.

'Bedwen looked up and laughed. "Pshaw!" she said, or something that sounded like that. "Did I wear *'bathers'* when I swam yesterday? The soldiers never wore *'bathers'* when they swam up here. Do you think I don't know what men look like?" There was an amused scorn in her voice.

'Are you going to swim too?' I asked, my heart thumping a bit in anticipation.

'Not today. Today I am making you a hat. Today I will watch *you* swim.' Then she added, 'If you can swim!'

'Actually, I was quite a good swimmer and often used to go to the Council-run swimming baths near where we lived in Birmingham. But this was to be a different kind of swim. Here was none of the echoey, chlorinated atmosphere of the indoor pool with shouting children and a po-faced supervisor walking round telling people off for splashing or pushing others in. Here was warm sunshine, sparkling water, almost absolute silence, apart from bird-calls, and a lovely young girl sitting cross-legged on the bank watching while she made me a hat out of reeds. And she was quite happy for me to swim with nothing on! Quite a heady mixture!'

CHAPTER FOUR

Sod's Law intervened at this point. Here I was, hanging on Tigerface's every word, and, before he could continue, the co-pilot came round to tell us all that the problem with the aircraft was now fixed and we were all to board immediately.

We finished our drinks, went out of the building and walked across the concrete to the aircraft. If we had thought it hot when we arrived, it was nothing to the heat now. It rose in shimmering waves from the concrete apron, making the aircraft and distant buildings appear and disappear. Fractious children were wailing and wimpering as they were hauled along by their mothers or carried by their fathers and helped up the steps and into the aircraft where it was a little cooler. But it was not really comfortable until the engines started and the fresh air system started to work. We taxied round and took off on the last leg of the flight.

Tigerface and I had the same seats as before and, when we had fastened our safety belts, I urged him to continue his story.

'Bedwen was making you a hat and you were about to have a swim,' I prompted him. 'But you didn't have any *bathers!*'

'Ah, yes. It was hot that day but nothing to what we've just put up with. Bedwen had her head down over the hat she was making so I went up to the top end of the pool, slipped off my shorts and waded in, keeping my back to where she was sitting. My coyness seems absurd now, especially as we would often swim together later on.

'However, I was more than a little embarrassed that day when I wanted to come out and get dry.'

I opened my mouth to ask the obvious question but Tigerface anticipated it.

'Yes, of course I did! I was just coming up to sixteen and the testosterone was playing havoc with me. Bits of moustache and beard were sprouting in the unscarred places on my face and my night-time dreams were running wild. She must have seen the effect she was having on me but, just as she had done when she first saw my face up close, she was always composed and never showed surprise or concern. I loved her for that as well.

'I dried myself with my shirt and pulled my shorts back on. The hat Bedwen was making was beginning to look like a hat and her fingers were plaiting and weaving the rushes so quickly that the movements were almost blurred. I picked more of the rushes and laid them on the grass where she could reach them as before. She would occasionally glance at my head as though judging the size and soon the crown was finished and the brim beginning to spread out. I kept topping up the pile of rushes until she had made a brim as wide as the one on her hat – but not as floppy. Then she turned up one side and, with a few quick movements of twisted rushes, secured it like that and laid it on the grass between us.

'Aren't you going to put it on?' she asked, as I hesitated.

'I picked it up, put in on and it fitted perfectly.'

'She looked at me and said, "I made it like the hats the Ost-raal-yun soldiers wore when they were at the camp. I thought that you would be happy with one like that."

'She pronounced the word just as the Aussies do and I realised that she would only ever have heard it spoken. There must have been Australian soldiers at the camp at some time. I assured her that I *was* very happy with that, stood up and paraded up and down like a soldier – wearing the hat she had just made for me. She smiled at first, then, when I gave myself marching commands in an Australian accent, she laughed out loud and said, "Good on yer," and it was my time to laugh.

'The sun was dropping towards the line of the hills to the west, neither of us had eaten anything and I remembered Aunt Becca and thought that she might be worrying about me, as I had never stayed away that long before. Perhaps reading my thoughts, Bedwen stood up, said that she must go and, to my delight, added, "If you can come earlier tomorrow, I will show you my castle and, if it is still a hot day again, we can swim together."

'The *"my castle"* was significant but I did not understand why and the prospect of us swimming together was thrilling to me. Wearing my new hat, I said something like, "Until tomorrow, then," and, despite wanting to kiss her goodbye, or at least shake her hand, I refrained and watched her walk away up the track and over the rise in the ground. I noticed that about half a dozen rather tame jackdaws who had been pecking about in the grass at the far end of the pool, rose up as she left and circled above her head, calling to each other as they flew.

'Once she was out of sight, I ran down the track, aware that, even then, my feet were not as tender as they had been before and, at the stile I put my shoes and socks on as I watched the landscape fade and change. I hid my hat where my shoes had been and hurried on down to the camp, expecting Aunt Becca to interrogate me the way Mum did if I came home later than expected. But all she said was, "Good lad. You're just in time for supper," – which is what she always called our evening meal.'

'In the morning, I rushed my chores, made a couple of sandwiches, put these in a bag with some apples and told Aunt Becca that I was going to the top of the valley to look at the castle I had seen there. If I had said anything like that to Mum she would have gone on about "Being careful" and "Not doing anything I shouldn't," which was understandable – but Aunt Becca just said, "See you later then, Dewi." She too, was now calling me by my Welsh name.

'I swapped my shoes and socks for my Aussie hat by the stile and almost ran up the track. I was learning how to spot and avoid the leaves of flat thistles in the short grass and my feet were already less painful if I trod on any small stones.

'Bedwen was waiting on the bridge and the jackdaws were picking about in the grass by the pool. After our greetings I asked what the Welsh name for a jackdaw was and she replied, 'Jac-do,' and I laughed and said, 'Not very different then.'

'Lots of Welsh words are like that,' she said and as the summer progressed, she taught me many more.

'Before we left the bridge, Bedwen suggested I left the pack of food under the bridge, "or the jac-dos will find it." We walked up towards the castle, with the birds flying above us as we walked. As we got nearer, I asked if the castle had a name.

'It's called Castell-y-bwlch,' she replied, 'It means castle of the pass.'

The pass through the cliffs was very clear now and I asked if the pass had a name.

'Bwlch-y-castell – pass of the castle!' she said and we both laughed. It was as if we had been friends all our lives.

'It wasn't a big castle, more like a watchtower. Built of big chunks of stone at the corners with smaller stones filling in between and making the walls. It was square, about four storeys high and with no moat or outbuildings.

The entrance door was about six feet up at the top of a wide cobbled ramp. Being the first castle I had ever seen, other than in picture books and films, I was not surprised that it was in good order – even the wooden door swung easily on its huge iron hinges but, apart from us, there was no one there.

'We went into a big, cool room with an arched stone ceiling and very small slotted windows high up in the walls. There was a stale, horsey smell that I didn't recognise then. On one wall were hayracks which suggested that horses had been kept there but there was no hay in the racks and no droppings on the floor. A month before I would not have noticed such things but, having discovered with the goats and the chickens that what goes in at one end, comes out at the other, and then has to be shovelled up, I was beginning to see things that a city boy like me would not normally be aware of.

'Around the walls were recesses with traces of candle grease in them and, in the corner of the room, was a low stone arch with a spiral staircase going up through the thickness of the wall. Bedwen led the way. At the first-floor level there was an opening into another room the same size as the one below with a big fireplace in one wall and a wooden table and benches in the centre and, as in the stable room below, there were recesses for candles in the walls. This room was different in that there were much larger, pointed-topped windows with wooden shutters, all of which were open, with a cool breeze blowing through them. Here the ceiling was wooden, supported on great timber beams set into the walls. There was no sign of any occupants and Bedwen again led the way up the spiral staircase and into the top room. This had a much lower ceiling but that was of stone like the one on the ground floor. Unlike the rooms below, this room had wooden partitions forming several smaller rooms within it, each one with a small square window with open shutters. There was a wide straight staircase leading up from the centre of this room through an opening in the stone ceiling and onto the castle roof. In the centre of the room near the foot of the staircase was a big stack of old, dry wood, which I worked out later, was fuel for a beacon on the roof.

'Bedwen pointed to the only room which had a closed door and said briefly, "That's my room," and went straight on up the staircase, with me following. At the top, she stepped out of a sort of stone porch and onto a flat roof covered in wide sheets of lead. The view was stunning. Not only could I look back down the whole of the valley I had come up, almost as far as the army camp but, in the other direction, I could see down another wide valley as deserted as the first. The track from my valley ran past the castle, through a narrow gap and on down the other side until it disappeared into woodland with a glimpse of fields beyond. As a vantage point to watch for movements up the track in either direction, it was unsurpassed.

'There was a parapet wall about four feet high all around the roof but what next caught my attention was a raised stone platform with a metal structure like a big basket on top of an iron post in the centre. Even a city boy like me could recognise that this building was a watch-tower and a signalling beacon, rather than a defensive castle but I could see how it could hold out for a good time if it *was* threatened by an enemy force.

'To either side were low cliffs forming the heads of both valleys but these were probably out of bowshot of the castle or they could have been used to shoot at people on the roof. Of course I wasn't thinking of these things at the time, just thrilled to be on the roof of an old castle in brilliant sunshine near to a girl I was deeply in love with, even if we had known each other for such a short time.'

Tigerface paused, his striped face glowing with the joy of his memories of that time and I wondered how many other people had heard this story and had wanted to believe it as much as I wanted to. The Britannia droned on, probably somewhere above the Mediterranean but Tigerface and I were standing on a castle roof, deep in the wilds of South Wales. I waited, eager for him to continue.

CHAPTER FIVE

Tigerface was still in some kind of reverie and, not knowing how much more he had to tell me, I again prompted him to continue. I would have hated to have the story cut short because our plane had landed and we had to go our separate ways. 'What happened then?' I asked gently.

Sod's law struck again. One of the crew was coming round offering drinks or even a meal – I can't remember which, and it doesn't matter anyway – the story and the mood had been interrupted.

However, when the trays had been cleared away, Tigerface took up his story again. 'We were up on the castle roof in the sunshine with a warm breeze blowing through the gap between the cliffs and a dozen or so jackdaws were playing on the wind where it was funnelled upwards by the walls of the tower. I was beginning to realise that whenever I was with Bedwen there were jackdaws about. Not intrusively so but always somewhere near. They would perch on the beacon and then fly out over the windward wall and be tossed up by the breeze high above our heads and then they would twist and spin down round the tower and back up to their perch again. Their joy was infectious and we watched them for a while, leaning against the parapet. I noticed that Bedwen still kept the four foot gap between us. She was again wearing the short green dress and her floppy brimmed hat, which she held on with one hand when the wind gusted. God –

she looked beautiful! It made me wonder how *I* looked to *her*. I was wearing the Aussie hat she had made for me but my face was an awful mess. One eyebrow was missing altogether, my nose was bent to the left, my jawbone, which had been broken in the smash, had set crooked and the gashes down either side of my face were far more noticeable than now. Yet she looked at me and smiled with no hint of concern or pity and I loved her even more for that.

'I would like to go and swim in the pool now,' she said, and I followed her down the stairs, my heart thumping with excitement. Leaving the castle and treading carefully down the ramp, we ran down the grassy track to the pool, Bedwen carrying her hat and with her hair streaming out behind her. I was a couple of yards behind her, carrying my Aussie hat and running as fast as I could but, however hard I ran, I couldn't catch up with her. I don't think I have ever been happier or felt more alive than I did in that run down to the pool. She had her dress off over her head as soon as we reached the grass patch and dived into the water whilst I was still unbuttoning my shorts. I jumped in, not being much good at diving and not knowing how deep the pool was.

'In the water, Bedwen kept the same sort of distance away from me as she always did on the land and I was beginning to accept that this was how it had to be. We swam about a bit, cooling off, even though the water was much warmer than I would have expected a mountain stream to be.'

Tigerface turned to me and said, 'If you ever get the chance to swim in a mountain stream in sunny weather, choose a wide, bowl-shaped valley like that one. In those valleys the rain water and the spring water moves slowly through the mossy bogs and warms up. Steep sided valleys always have cold water. Worst of all are those where the valley has been dammed and the stream comes out of the foot of the dam – they're damned cold.'

It wasn't a very good joke but he was right – as I have found out in the years since. I wanted him to get back to his story as I was eager to know more and be able to judge whether he was telling the truth or just entertaining me with a male fantasy.

After a brief pause Tigerface went on, 'I stayed in the water to give Bedwen a chance to get out when *she* was ready, and she may have been doing the same for me. But, when I was finding myself a bit chilled, I climbed up the bank and sat in the sun watching Bedwen as she followed me out. I know I've said before how beautiful she was but it was more than that. If you ever saw an antelope leaping or a wild horse galloping in open country, or even a kestrel hovering, you will know that certain creatures have a beauty of movement that is hard to describe. Bedwen had that beauty – especially when she was naked. I used to think of it as barefoot all over!

'We dried in the sun wearing just our hats until there came a time when it seemed natural to put our clothes on and I retrieved the pack of sandwiches and apples from the ledge under the bridge. We shared these, with me leaving the open pack on the ground between us and Bedwen reaching for hers from the pack.

'A pair of wagtails were pecking about in the grass for insects, as were the jackdaws, and a dipper came flitting up the stream, alighting on a stone by the pool and then diving into the water with scarcely a splash. All of this was exciting and new to me – remember only a week or two before I had never even been out of the city. I asked Bedwen why it had dived into the pool and she said, "That's where it finds its food. It eats insects that live at the bottom of the pool." She got up, lifted a stone from the water and showed me little tubes made of grains of sand with tiny legs sticking out of one end. "Those are what it eats," she said, putting the stone gently back into the same place that she had taken it from. "If the birds or the fish don't eat them they turn into little flies later in the year."

'The dipper flew out from the bushes at the top end of the pool where I had found its nest and flew up the stream to get more water insects. While it was away, Bedwen showed me the babies in the nest with their wide-open beaks, thinking that we were their mother coming back with more food. I wanted to somehow capture the vision of that tiny nest tucked safely up in secret hollow under that overhanging rock and decided that I would make a drawing of it to show Aunt Becca after I got back that evening.

'Then Bedwen and I walked on up the side of the stream with her pointing out many things I wouldn't have noticed if I had been on my own. There were clumps of cotton-grass with fluffy white tufts halfway up their stems and sundew plants with sticky pads to catch insects which they dissolved and 'ate'. Everything we saw was known to Bedwen and she seemed to get pleasure in showing them to me and telling me all about them and, for most of that summer we roamed around the valley while she taught me all about the plants and the animals and the birds that lived there.

'That evening I told Aunt Becca about the dipper's nest and asked if she had any paper so that I could draw it to show her. I used to be quite good at Art in school but now I found that my hand shook when I was holding a pencil. Probably something to do with the nerves in my arm from the crash and what I drew was disappointingly poor and I said so.

'Aunt Becca looked at the picture and asked, "Can you take photographs?"

'I had never used a camera – one of my friends had a Box Brownie but film was quite expensive and then you had to pay for the films to be developed and printed. I told her "No" and she asked if I would like to learn. Of course, I said I would and wondered what she had in mind. Cameras and disused Army camps being used as farm buildings didn't seem to go together but Aunt Becca went into her bedroom and came back carrying a small black leather pack. After a bit of fumbling with a catch, she opened the front and pulled out what she called the bellows – you will have seen those on old fashioned cameras?'

I had and I knew that a camera with bellows was not a child's toy but a piece of very expensive equipment.

'This belonged to my fiancé. Danny was very keen on photography before... before... before the war,' she said. 'I'm sure he wouldn't mind if you used it now.'

'This was the first time she had mentioned having been engaged and I knew enough about the war and people being killed, not to follow this up.'

'He left this here," she said, 'and a box of films. You can have these if you like – *I'm* not going to need them.'

'I took the camera and films and carefully tried out all the levers and buttons, working out what each one did, then opened the back and found out how to put a film in, remembering to do this in dim light. My friend with the camera had told me about that. While I was doing that Aunt Becca went into her bedroom and came back with a beautiful light-weight folding tripod and a flexible cord about a foot long which screwed over the shutter button. This had another button on the end and when you pressed it the shutter worked without any danger of the camera shaking.'

Tigerface looked at me a touch apologetically. 'I hope I'm not boring you with all this detail but these extra bits were perfect for what I wanted the camera for. It was as if all that gear had all been left there just for me. Of course it hadn't – I was just lucky!

'Anyway, the next day I took the camera and tripod with me when I went to meet Bedwen. She asked what it was for and, when I told her it was to make pictures of birds and animals, she said that I must *not* take pictures of her. She said this in the same way as she had said that I mustn't touch her and I just accepted this.'

Tigerface turned to me and asked, 'Back in Kenya, did you find that the Africans hated having their photos taken? They believed that you were taking away a part of themselves, or a part of their lives. I never worked out quite what, but one had to respect that.

'Anyway, I set up the camera, on the tripod, by the dipper's nest and took a photo of the babies with their wide open beaks but not really knowing how it would come out. I took a lot of photos that summer of animals and birds and plants without seeing any of the results until I got back to Birmingham and had them developed and printed. I was quite prepared for them all to be rubbish but many of them were quite good. One odd thing was that any pictures I had taken of the castle were all fuzzy, even though some were on different rolls of film and *all* the ones of birds and animals were fine. I never quite worked out why.

'So that's how my *Barefoot Summer* passed. Roaming around that magical valley with a beautiful girl who I knew I must not touch, watching and learning about the wildlife, taking photos that may or may not come out, while all the time my body and mind were recovering from that awful car crash. Bedwen taught me the Welsh names of the birds, the animals and the trees. When she told me that a birch tree was *Bedwen* it seemed very appropriate. Birch trees were as beautiful and as graceful as my Bedwen, who needless to say, I was growing to love more and more each day.'

CHAPTER SIX

Our flight must have been somewhere over France at that time and I could sense that Tigerface's story of his Barefoot Summer must be coming to an end and I wondered just how he could leave the valley and Bedwen – but there was more to come.

'On Coronation Day – you remember this was 1953 – Aunt Becca had asked if I wanted to go with her and her friend down to Abergavenny but I had said, "No thank you," not wanting to miss a day with Bedwen. We met at the pool as we usually did, and then went up to the castle and sat on the roof enjoying the warm breeze. I told Bedwen about it being Coronation Day and she asked who was to be crowned. I said, "Queen Elizabeth, of course!" She asked me what Queen Elizabeth looked like and I remembered the crown coin Mum had given me but which I hadn't really looked at since then. It was in the back pocket of my shorts where I kept it as a sort of reminder of Mum and Dad but, to be honest, I didn't think about them very much – they lived in another world – or perhaps it was me who was in the other world!

'I took the coin out to show Bedwen the Queen's head but it wasn't there. On one side was a distant view of the Queen riding side-saddle on a horse and on the other side were four shields and a crown. I turned it back over to make sure, as all other coins I had ever seen had a king or a queen's head on one side, and as I did that I dropped it on the lead roof where it flashed in the sunshine as it rolled down the gentle slope.

'One of the jackdaws dived down from the beacon, snatched up the coin before it had finished rolling and flew over the parapet with the coin in its beak. I shouted and ran to see where it had gone but the bird and the coin had vanished. Completely vanished!

'I leaned over the parapet expecting to see the bird flying away but there was no sign of it. I turned towards Bedwen, who was coming across the roof to look and, when I turned back, the bird *was* flying away from the castle, about ten or fifteen feet below me. It was not carrying the coin and had obviously come out of a window in one of the rooms on the floor below. I asked Bedwen if there were any jackdaw's nests in any of the rooms and she said that she was sure there were not. I followed her down the stairs and we searched the four rooms on the side of the tower where I had seen the bird fly away from. On that side, there were two rooms on either side of the stairway but there was no sign of a nest or any other hiding place in any of these. Of course, my mind was full of thoughts about thieving jackdaws and the old poem we had read at school about The Jackdaw of Rheims who stole the bishop's ring.

'To be honest, the coin was not that important to me but I was intrigued as to where it had been hidden. I thought that there must be a crack in the outer wall below the staircase and Bedwen and I went down to ground level and walked right around the castle. There were five small square windows at the top level on all four walls, but we knew there were only four rooms on one side, two each side of the stairs. Could there be a hidden room *under* the stairs? We ran back up the inside staircases – that shows how fit I was then – and searched for the door to that room – but there wasn't one. Bedwen was as puzzled as I was, although this castle was obviously her home. I thought that one of the stone steps must lift up but none of them did. Then we looked on each side of the stairway to see if there were any secret doors or signs that one might have been blocked up at some time, but we drew a blank there too. There was just a recess about eighteen inches square and a foot or so deep on either side to hold a candlestick as there were in all the other rooms, so we went back up on the roof to think. I leaned over the parapet above the middle widow but there was no way down there without a rope, so I went downstairs again and had another look. The secret must be in the candle recesses and I tapped the vertical flat stone at the back of each with a stick from the log pile. One definitely sounded more hollow than the other and I poked at the side of that stone with the end of the stick and it moved a bit sideways.

'With Bedwen standing behind me – still at a careful distance – I prised the stone sideways and it soon slid easily in a hidden groove to leave an opening that I thought I could wriggle through. A draught of musty air came out of the hole – I don't know if you've ever smelt a jackdaw's nest – they stink of old droppings and sheep's wool. I could see inside as that room under the stairs *did* have a window opening just like the other rooms, but with no shutters.

'I stepped back to let Bedwen see and she asked me if I was going in to find my coin. It never entered my head then that it might be a trap of some kind. I suppose I thought it was more like a kind of priest's hole for somebody to hide in. Anyway, I did wriggle through head-first and dropped onto a mass of twigs and metallic objects that moved slightly as I landed with my arms outstretched. I picked up one of the objects and it was a metal cartridge case, green with a sort of patina but at one time, it must have been shiny bright. There were thousands of these, obviously collected by the jackdaws when the valley was a firing range during the war. I passed a couple through the hole to Bedwen and she called back and asked if had found my coin. In the excitement at being in the hidden room, I had forgotten about that and started to look for it. Then I started to find other things amongst the cartridge cases. There were many coins, lots of rings – some with glittering stones in them –and several pretty brooches. The more I riffled through the cartridges the more treasures I found. There were also a lot of aluminium foil milk-bottle tops so I knew the jackdaws must have been collecting their hoard from a huge area as people for many miles around only drank fresh milk from their own cows or goats.

'As I gathered each handful of trinkets and coins, I passed these through to Bedwen and went on searching. Eventually I found my crown-piece where it had slipped down through the cartridges and, next to it, I found an exquisite little brooch enamelled in bright green and in the shape of a birch tree. Remembering that Bedwen's name meant 'Birch tree' in Welsh, I slipped the brooch into the back pocket of my shorts together with my crown coin. One last check through the rubbish to make sure that I had taken everything of value and I wriggled back through the hole on my tummy and slid down, headfirst and with arms outstretched, onto the floor.

'Bedwen must have fetched a basket from her room as there was one on the floor beside her, almost full with the things I had passed out to her. "Did you find your coin?" she asked and when I patted my back pocket, she asked, in a plaintive sort of way, "Was that *everything*?"

'Not quite," I said teasingly and carried the basket of goodies up on to the roof where we sat on the stone base of the beacon with the basket between us. It was bright and hot up there and we put our hats on to shade our eyes. Bedwen's face was gleaming with anticipation and I took the birch-tree brooch out of my pocket and laid it on top of the other items in the basket.

'So they *did* take it!' she said and I noticed for the first time that there were no jackdaws on the roof now.

She took off her hat, picked up the brooch and pinned it on the side of the hat, where it looked perfectly at home – if you understand what I mean.'

The memory of that moment was clearly important to Tigerface as he paused for a minute, taking a handkerchief out of his pocket and pretending to be blowing his nose, although I could see that he was really wiping away a tear or two before he could speak again. I looked out of the plane's window while he composed himself and then he said, 'I asked Bedwen, "What are we going to do with all of this?" I was vaguely aware that there were rules on treasure trove and lost items that one had found. "Do whatever you like," she said carelessly and it was clear that she only cared about the brooch. "We *could* put them back in the jackdaws' room."

'I didn't like that idea. Even though Bedwen seemed to have no interest in the coins and the jewellery – other than the brooch – and only the crown coin was mine, I still felt that we had discovered hidden treasure and it should be used in some way.

'What about the jackdaws?" I asked. 'Won't they just take the things away and hide them somewhere else?'

Bedwen's anwer was immediate. "We *won't* put them back. If they take things that don't belong to them they can't expect to keep them!" She had taken her hat off and was stroking the brooch with her fingers. "*They* can keep all the other things –the bits that spit out of the guns *and* the shiny disks! I'll keep *these* safe in my room."

'I had never been in her room and didn't know how safe that would be but I didn't care too much. The coins were interesting and the jewellery was pretty but I had no idea of their real value. We spent a couple of hours that afternoon laying it all out in rows on the stone base of the beacon – as I said, there were no jackdaws about now. There were dozens of rings, brooches and pendants – some very old-fashioned looking and about a bucketful of coins with dates from the fifteen-hundreds up to the 1950s. Bedwen admired much of the jewellery but only the birch tree brooch, now pinned to her hat, really interested her. In the end, we put all the pieces and the coins back in the basket, which Bedwen lugged into her room and shut the door so that I could not see in.

'We had our swim later than usual that day, as exciting and joyous as usual, but the air was cooling as I ran back down to the stile, put my shoes and socks on and hid my Aussie hat as I normally did. I was not expecting Aunt Becca to be home by then from the Coronation celebrations in Abergavenny as she had asked me to milk the goats that evening. However, she *was* there and looking worried, not like someone who had enjoyed a special day out with a friend.

Tigerface half-turned and said, 'I don't think I'd told you that the postman didn't come up to the farm with our post but left it in a box at the end of the lane. Aunt Becca or I fetched it a couple of times a week. There was never much post anyway.

'I asked her what was the matter and she passed me a letter in an open brown envelope with O. H. M. S. printed at the top. She obviously intended me to read it so I did. It was from the War Office and declared that "As she appeared to have no intention of vacating Talybwlch Training Base (formerly Talybwlch Farm), the Secretary of State, after receiving representations on her behalf from her solicitors, Messrs Evans, Evans and Evans, had decided to grant her a lifetime tenancy for the sum of £500 per year, back-dated for four years. The four years being the time it had taken to reach this conclusion. Much more legal guff followed about making good any damage, etc.etc. Much of it meant little to me but, when I looked up, Aunt Becca was crying – and that really upset me.

'Where do they expect me to find £2,000?' she asked. 'The damned lawyers have taken any money I had and my nurse's pension is tiny.'

'I thought of the £20 or so I had in my Post Office savings account back in Birmingham and would have given her all of that willingly but that was obviously no good. Then I remembered the treasure Bedwen and I had found. I thought at the time that this was an amazing coincidence but my main concern was whether it was real or not and, if I promised it to Aunt Becca, would it really be there the next day. I decided not to say anything about it and handed the letter back with some kind of bland statement like, "Something will come up." But I was torn as to whether I should say more.

'That night my dreams were full of treasure, pieces of eight and golden doubloons, being counted under a palm tree on a sandy beach by a girl who sometime wore a green dress and a straw hat with a floppy brim but, to be honest, mostly wore only the hat. I was fifteen at the time, remember!'

I smiled, remembering my dreams when I was fifteen.

'And then...' I prompted, desperate to hear the end of this story before we landed at Stanstead.

CHAPTER SEVEN

The events I am relating here took place over half a century ago. When Tigerface was telling me about finding the treasure just as Aunt Becca's money problems came to a head, I thought, 'That's one hell of a coincidence!'

Now that I am very much older and perhaps a little wiser, I am ready to believe that Tigerface, Bedwen, Aunt Becca and even the jackdaws were all caught up in an exquisitely elegant synchronistic experience.

Tigerface picked up my prompt. 'And then – the next day I did my chores, packed a double lunch as usual and went up to the castle, leaving my shoes and socks hidden near the stile and putting on my Aussie hat. It had rained in the night and the air was fresh and clear and the grass cool and moist under my bare feet. Bedwen was waiting at the bridge by the pool and I noticed immediately that she was wearing the birch-tree brooch on the side of her hat. I said, "Hello," desperately wanting to kiss her but knowing that this was not allowed under the rules of that summer in that valley.

'She quickly picked up my mood of concern and soon had me telling her about Aunt Becca's letter.

'She can have the things the jackdaws stole,' she said. 'Except for this one!' She touched the brooch on her hat. I was still unsure if the "things" were real and was afraid that they might disappear if I took them out of the valley. Bedwen didn't seem to know either so we decided to try it out with one coin and one ring. We selected a gold coin with the head of George III on it and a pretty little ring with a brown stone that glowed as if it had a hidden light behind it. On either side of that stone were two shiny white ones that I guessed were diamonds. I put the ring and the coin in the back pocket of my shorts and Bedwen fetched the camera from 'her room' where she kept it each night to save me carrying it up each day. We, or at any rate me, then forgot about Aunt Becca and her problems and spent the rest of the morning as usual with Bedwen showing me how to get close to wild animals and birds to photograph them.

'I think it might have been a hare that day. Anyway, when the sun was high we had our swim in the pool and we shared my lunch sitting on the bridge as we dried in the sunshine naked, as we often did. Then Bedwen said, "You should go now and show your aunt the things we chose for her." I was reluctant to go so soon but knew that the next day would be the same so I agreed, dressed and waved goodbye to her as I went off down the track.

'Aunt Becca had taken her loom out of the guardroom and set it up in the shade on the veranda. She was threading the warps – or were those the wefts? Anyway, it doesn't matter – one or the other – and was surprised to see me back so early. "Are you alright?" she asked, as I stood beside where she was sitting.

'Before I replied, I took the coin and the ring out of my pocket and was relieved – very relieved – to find that they were still there and felt just as solid as they did up at the castle. I had half-expected them to melt away to nothing in my hand. I held the coin out to show Aunt Becca and she took it and turned it over and over. "From the castle?" she asked and I said, "Yes. Bedwen and I found it where the jackdaws had hidden it."

'This was the first time I had mentioned Bedwen to Aunt Becca and I waited for a reaction. Had I broken some kind of spell? Would all the magic of the valley float away? I went cold at the thought. It was still only early June and the thought of spending the next few months without Bedwen at my side was devastating, but Aunt Becca just said, "Isn't she beautiful! When I was a girl, we used to play together up at the castle – and swim in the pool by the bridge. I expect you do that."

'Something in my mind told me that there must be some mistake – Aunt Becca was the same age as my mother, which was about forty, and Bedwen was my age, or close to it, so she couldn't have been born when Aunt Becca was a girl. Like so many things to do with Aunt Becca, Bedwen, the valley and the castle, none of the usual time-scales seemed to apply. But Aunt Becca had seen the ring that I was still holding and held out her hand to take it. As I gave it to her it was the first time that I noticed that the stone between the two diamonds on the ring exactly matched the warm honey colour of her eyes.

'I forgot about mixed-up times then for Aunt Becca was holding the ring and crying. For a boy it is always disturbing when a grown-up cries in front of you. She then put it on the third finger of her left hand, got up from her working stool and hugged me. "Oh, David," she said. "This is my engagement ring. Those damned jackdaws must have taken it soon after Danny..." Her words tailed off into sniffs.

'She held me tight against her for enough time for me to start to feel uncomfortable about it. I think she might have held me close for so long so that I couldn't see her crying but her whole body was shaking. When she did let me go, she kissed my scarred forehead twice and said, "Thank you, thank you, thank you." All very emotional for a fifteen year old who was a bit unused to shows of family affection!

'Still wearing the ring, she went back to threading the wool in her loom and I sat and watched her. After a couple of minutes she asked, a bit hesitantly, "Did you and Bedwen find anything else?"

'I could see what she was thinking and said, "There were lots of other coins and rings and things. Bedwen doesn't want them. If I brought them down here we could sell them to pay the rent money."

'Aunt Becca didn't reply at once. I could see that she was working out the legal and moral implications. Then she asked, 'Were these things old or new?"

'I couldn't really answer that regarding the jewellery but said that lots of the coins were old, as I could tell by the dates, and she said that, if they *were* old, they probably didn't belong to anyone and we *could* sell them. She told me not to mention what we had found to anyone else while she made sure – which was a bit unnecessary as I only saw her and Bedwen – and Bedwen knew all about them anyway. I only wrote to Mum about once a week and there was no way I could tell her without also telling her about Bedwen and a lot of other things she would never understand.'

CHAPTER EIGHT

I was suddenly aware of a change of note from the aircraft engines. A wing dipped slightly and, when I looked out of the window, I could see that one of the propellers had been feathered. At the same time, Chalky's professionally calm voice announced that there was a slight problem with an overheating bearing in one engine and, as a precaution, they were 'resting' it and would fly on with the other three.

I knew he could fly this lightly loaded plane perfectly well with just two engines if need be and said this to Tigerface, who was looking a little concerned, perhaps connected with his boyhood experience with the aero engine in the stream. I also knew that this malfunction would delay our arrival and was secretly pleased about that. I wanted to hear the end of Tigerface's story and this would give us more time. I still wasn't sure if I believed half of what he was telling me – however much I wanted to!

The crew had been preparing a cooked meal and brought it round at once – a useful diversion for any nervous passengers. Tigerface and I ate ours in silence but as soon as the trays were taken away, I asked a question to restart his story. 'Did your Aunt sell the coins and things?'

'Oh, yes. The next day I took an old kitbag up to the castle and Bedwen filled it with the coins and the jewellery. I was so excited and eager to give them to Aunt Becca that I even went without our swim! Aunt Becca was even more excited than me as we laid them out on the table and sorted them into piles. I arranged the coins in date order and Aunt Becca sorted the jewellery stuff by what she considered was century by century. I couldn't help her with that but she seemed to know what she was doing. Then she took a sample from each pile to show someone she knew when she next went to Abergavenny.

'As far as I was concerned,' Tigerface said, 'I didn't mind what happened to them if Aunt Becca was happy again and I could go on swimming with Bedwen and learning from her how to get close enough to the animals and birds to get really good photographs. She taught me so much – how to stalk them up-wind, how to move when their heads were down as they fed and how to freeze instantly when they looked up. Mostly I learned not to be in a hurry – but that was easy as, if we had to stay still for a long time, I just looked at Bedwen and adored her silently.

'Aunt Becca must have been selling the coins and things surreptitiously because she was suddenly happy again and sang welsh folk-songs as she fed the goats. I learned that the welsh for goat is *gafr* and now, whenever I hear someone refer to their boss as "gaffer", I have a little smile to myself.

'The rest of the summer passed in much the same way. My face had healed and I was strong and fit and knew that soon I would have to go back to Brum and face the string of operations to make it reasonably presentable.'

Tigerface turned to look at me. 'It took nearly two years on and off but I think the surgeons did a pretty good job – don't you?'

This was an invitation to look closely at his face, which I had avoided until then for fear of giving offence. Apart from the residual and still slightly shiny scars, it was a handsome face with clear blue eyes that looked straight at one. Was it my imagination that read regret and sadness there? His jaw, which I knew had been reset, was prominent and strong and I wondered briefly if that how it had always been or had the surgeon been especially kind?

'Brilliant!' I said. 'A first class job!' But I really wanted to hear how his *Barefoot Summer* had ended. How did he part from the lovely Bedwen? Did he ever see her again?

Tigerface must have anticipated this for he said, 'You must be wondering how it all ended?'

'I hope you're going to tell me,' I said, invitingly.

'Well, like all good things in this life, it *had* to end,' he said. 'A day in late August had been set for Dad to come down and collect me and that day rushed up on me. It had been the most amazing summer for weather. The only times it had rained had been at night – and then just enough to keep the countryside green and the farmers' crops growing well. I had a box full of undeveloped films, which I was looking forward to seeing, but my main concern was leaving Bedwen on her own up at the castle. I was conceited enough to believe that she would miss me as much as I knew I was going to miss her and, although I never thought it through, I knew we could not write to one another. My only hope was that I could come back the next year.

'The dreaded day came. Dad was due at about midday and I got up early, skipped my chores by agreement with Aunt Becca and went up to the pool, leaving my shoes and socks hidden for the last time. It was gloriously sunny and Bedwen was waiting for me even at that time. She must have anticipated that I would come earlier than usual.

I had brought some welsh-cakes that Aunt Becca had made for me. Flat round cakes, full of sultanas, which she knew I loved. Bedwen and I shared them as we sat on the parapet of the bridge and as soon as we had eaten them, Bedwen threw down her hat, drew her dress over her head with the movement that always fascinated me and ran across the grass and into the pool. I stripped off and followed, gasping as the water had not yet been warmed by the sun. We neither of us stayed in for long and we then ran up and down the grass to warm up. Then I did the stupidest thing I have ever done in my whole stupid life! I forgot the 'no touching' rule and hugged her.

There was a moment of exquisite sensual joy and then she was gone!

'Where she had been standing was a birch tree that I was sure had not been there a second before. In fact, I knew it hadn't been there! It was a graceful young tree, not quite as tall as I was. I knew it was my fault that she wasn't there anymore but before I left the pool I called out her name again and again and even apologised to the tree – but I really knew it was useless and this was the end!

I was crying unashamedly as I put my shorts and shirt on, picked up her green dress and her hat with the brooch pinned to it and walked up to the castle carrying them. Upstairs I opened the door to what she had called her room and I had never before seen inside. It was empty – completely bare – but swept clean. With my last forlorn hope dashed, I looked around to see where I should leave her hat and her dress? I couldn't just leave them in that empty room where anyone might find them so I slid back the stone to the secret room. I unpinned the birch tree brooch from her hat, nestled her hat inside mine and wrapped them both in her dress. I kissed the bundle, reached in through the hole in the wall and dropped it on the cartridge cases below. I put the brooch carefully in my pocket and slid the stone back in place.

'I walked down to the grassy place by the pool, stroked the leaves of the birch tree, whispered a ''goodbye' and a 'thank you' and ran down to the stile.

As I put on my shoes and socks, I watched the scenery mystically change for the last time and knew that my magical *Barefoot Summer* was finally over.

'Dad had not arrived when I got back and Aunt Becca said nothing about the castle or Bedwen and that was fine by me – we didn't need to spell these things out. I folded the birch tree brooch in the special blanket that Aunt Becca had made for me and I had slept under every day I had been there, and rolled it up before putting it in my suitcase.

'I was going round saying goodbye to the goats and the chickens just as Dad arrived, in a panic as before and frantic to get back to the city that he understood. I had a quick hug from Aunt Becca and Dad grabbed my suitcase and put it in the taxi.

'No word from Dad about my appearance, only a brief and seemingly insincere *thank you* from him to Aunt Becca and we were off down the track!

CHAPTER NINE

Just at that time Chalky walked down the aisle with a brief word to any of the passengers who seemed to need reassurance. As he reached the row where Tigerface and I were sitting, I asked him if we had an E.T.A. and he glanced momentarily out of the window at the idle propeller and said, "We should be landing in about two hours," and moved off down the aircraft.

Tigerface was sitting quietly looking ahead as though that was the end of the story. I wanted to know more and asked, 'What did your Mum say when you got home?'

Tigerface started as though his thoughts had been elsewhere and he replied, 'Oh, you know the sort of thing. "It's nice to have you home." "How well you look." "How was Aunt Becca?" That sort of thing.'

I wondered about the brooch and asked him if he still had it and he said, 'Well, that was a funny thing. When I got back to Brum and took my suitcase into my rooms to unpack it, the blanket was there but the brooch wasn't. I checked everything, even my pockets but no brooch! I could only think that Aunt Becca had taken it out of my case when I was out with the goats. I didn't know why and I was disappointed. I thought of mentioning this in my letter thanking her for having me all summer but decided not to. I didn't mention Bedwen or the castle either.'

Tigerface was silent again and then he asked if I would like to see the actual brooch. Of course I said, 'Yes,' and he reached into an inside pocket and took out a little leather-covered box which he handed to me. After what I had heard in the last few hours, I handled it with great care and respect. The brooch was obviously his most treasured possession and meant as much to him as a piece of the True Cross would mean to a devout Christian or the tooth of the Buddha to a Buddhist monk visiting the temple in Sri Lanka where it is kept.

The box had been made for some other item of jewellery and within it nestled a small brooch in the shape of a birch tree with tiny enamelled leaves set in an exquisite silver mount. I didn't dare touch it but Tigerface took back the box and lifted the brooch out for me to hold and admire.

'Isn't it lovely!' he said – a statement not a question – and I had to agree. Then I wondered how he had it now. A few minutes ago he had said that it had disappeared out of his suitcase when he left Wales some ten or so years before, so I asked him how it had come to him and he said, 'I often planned to go down to Wales to see Aunt Becca again but I kept putting it off. I suppose I wanted to hang onto all my memories of that summer with Bedwen and was afraid of finding reality was less than I remembered. Then, out of the blue, I got a letter from Evans, Evans and Evans, who I remembered were the solicitors in Abergavenny who had acted for Aunt Becca when she was fighting the War office over possession of the old army camp.

'I sort of knew what it would say. Both my Mum and Dad had died in the last couple of years – Dad from liver failure and Mum from cancer – so I was not surprised to learn that Aunt Becca had died too, even though she was only about fifty. Early deaths were more common then. Anyway, the letter said that Aunt Becca had died and left everything to me and would I be able to come to their offices and arrange for the disposal of her 'effects'. They added that the Ministry of Defence had, shortly after her death, instructed them to remove all her possessions from Talybwlch Training Base which they now intended to demolish in accordance with the agreement made ... etcetera, etcetera, blah, blah, blah.

'When I got to Abergavenny there was not much to be done. The funeral was over by the time I got there. The solicitors had arranged for the livestock – the goats and the chickens – to be sold immediately in the market and apart from a healthy bank balance – which I guessed had come from the sale of the jackdaws' treasure – there was only a small brooch which her will had said was definitely to be personally given to me. I asked about the engagement ring and was told that she had left instructions that it was to be buried with her. I hoped her undertakers were honest men!

'I showed them my passport to confirm my identity, took *this* brooch and signed a receipt for it, gave them my bank details and went to visit Aunt Becca's grave at Groesvaen. It was a bleak day in a bleak Welsh village churchyard and I didn't stay long. Stupidly I drove up to Talybwlch where I briefly watched a JCB tearing down the huts, before parking out of the way and walking up to the castle. The pool was just the same as before and the lone birch tree in the grass patch seemed about the same size as it had been ten years earlier. Looking around to ensure that no one was watching I took off my shoes and socks and tried to bring back the magic of that Barefoot Summer – but I really knew it had gone for good. I put my shoes back on and walked up to the castle, which was not as it had been. High up on the front wall was a faded sign in red paint on a white board which must have been put there when the Army Camp was in operation but I knew was not there when Bedwen and I were there. It read BY ORDER OF THE WAR OFFICE. THIS BUILDING IS OUT OF BOUNDS TO ALL MILITARY PERSONNEL.

'The notice board was riddled with bullet holes which showed how much the soldiers had respected that authority and inside the castle the walls of the rooms were covered in sets of initials and crudely scratched insignias of various army units, one of which had a kangaroo motif. Empty cigarette packets and old paper bags littered the floor and the whole place reeked of decay. All the wooden partitions in the top room had gone –probably burned in the fireplace below, and much of the roof parapet had been pushed over and lay on the ground below. The iron beacon was gone, leaving just a rusty projecting stump of metal where the base had been set in the stone roof. I tried to slide the stone back in the wall which opened on to the secret room but it wouldn't move and I was glad of that. I didn't like the idea of anyone finding Bedwen's and my hats and her dress, even though they must have rotted away years before.

'I didn't stay long but went sadly down the valley, waved to the man on the JCB and drove off down the lane. And that's how I got the brooch.'

'Have you shown it to anyone else?' I asked feeling that I had been especially privileged to have handled something so obviously precious to him.

'Only Daniel M'wangi,' he replied. 'And that was just last week. I also told him the story that I've spent most of this flight boring you with.'

'I wasn't bored for a moment,' I assured him but did not add that I found much of it hard to believe and had already decided that he had made up most of it. Perhaps he was a frustrated raconteur and had found Daniel M'wangi and me to be conveniently captive audiences. I asked him what Daniel M'wangi had said when he heard it.

'He was a little drunk. He had been into the local village in the Land Rover to get supplies and had been sampling the locally brewed pombe.'

I knew about pombe – it was, and I suspect still is – a strong beer brewed from bananas or maize. Very potent stuff and Daniel M'wangi was a fool to drive after even one mugful of that.

'When he got back to camp he saw the brooch in my hand and asked what it was. I told him the same story as I have told you and he sat there by the fire as it got dark and listened intently. I wondered how he visualised castles and Welsh towns, as these would have been alien to him but, as his father had been a missionary, it was probable that he had seen picture books when he was a boy.

'When I finished he said something surprising – probably because he was still a bit under the influence of the pombe. He said, "Tell me Bwana. Do you still love the girl who you are calling Bedwen?" He didn't often call me Bwana – I preferred David, or even Tigerface, so I knew he was going to say something important and leaned forward to hear it.

'I replied that of course I did – I could never love anyone else – but that she had gone and could never come back.

'Daniel M'wangi burped, apologised and said very seriously, "Then you must pray to the God who lives up on Kerinyaga, the mountain that you call Mount Kenya. My father, may he rest in peace, told me that this God is *all mighty* and if you want something enough and pray hard enough, and you have enough love in your heart, your prayers will be answered. But it is important that you are facing the mountain when you pray or God won't be able to hear you."

'I thought that if this God was *all mighty* then it shouldn't matter which way you were facing but I didn't say so. I just packed him off to make our evening meal.'

'And *did* you pray?' I asked Tigerface, regretting it immediately. He may have taken me into his confidence with his story of his Barefoot Summer but in those days, well brought-up people avoided talking about religious beliefs. My own beliefs at the time were shaky to say the least, even though I dutifully attended R.A.F. church-parades and often chatted to the camp padre.

'No, of course not,' Tigerface replied rather shortly. 'I've no time for that sort of nonsense!'

Then I surprised myself by saying, 'Perhaps it could be worth a try. If I loved a girl as much as you love Bedwen, I'd try anything – even praying!'

Tigerface did not reply and I thought I had overstepped the unwritten bounds of our relationship. I was about to apologise when I saw that his eyes were closed so I said nothing. He must have been as tired as I was, after being in transit one way or another for nearly twenty-four hours. Then I saw that his lips were moving and he was holding Bedwen's brooch in his hand. I realised that, as all the passenger seats in R.A.F. aircraft face backwards for safety reasons, he was actually facing Mount Kenya and I wondered – *was* he praying?

I must have dropped off to sleep myself then, as I was woken by an announcement telling us we were shortly going to land in England and to fasten our seat belts. A ragged cheer went up from the other passengers and I glanced at Tigerface. He was awake and the brooch was no longer in his hand – he must have put it away while I was asleep. Chalky's disembodied voice then said, 'However, the bad news is that we have been diverted from Stanstead to Heathrow and we will be landing there.' He might have said why but I don't remember – probably something to do with the engine problem.

'It's been a long flight,' Tigerface said in a casual voice and I could tell that he had not taken offence at my earlier rudeness. 'It'll be good to be down and even better to be home.'

I wondered where home was for him but didn't ask. I was thinking about how to organise *my* onward journey as my journey plans had been thrown into disarray by the holdups on the flight and now by this diversion.

CHAPTER TEN

We landed normally and went through the usual passport checks and the reclamation of baggage routines and it was there I lost touch with Tigerface. It was probable that he had to make special arrangements for his camera and film equipment. When I was clear and had my bags and cases loaded onto a trolley, I went to the information desk and found that my best way home from Heathrow was on a coach that would not leave for another two and a half hours, so I stashed my trolley and went to the cafeteria to buy a drink. I walked stiffly over to the counter to order a strong coffee and saw Tigerface sitting about twenty feet away, sideways on to me, and knew that he had not yet seen me. There was a bit if a queue and I stood there patiently – I had some time to kill and I was glad to be standing up for a change. What I saw then really made me wonder.

A fair-haired woman of about my age came through the door, looked around and made her way directly towards the table where Tigerface sat alone. She was wearing a very chic green dress which just reached her knees and a floppy-brimmed straw hat. Without thinking, I glanced at her feet, almost expecting her to be barefoot and dismissed the idea as nonsense. In fact, she was wearing a smart pair of shoes in a green colour that matched her dress. She must have seen me looking at her and gave me a look which clearly said, 'You keep out of this,' and I saw that her eyes were that very rare violet colour that immediately made me think of Elizabeth Taylor as I had seen her in *National Velvet*, aged about twelve or thirteen, and, more recently, in Cat on a Hot Tin Roof. The woman then ignored me and stood by the table where Tigerface was sitting and fondling what I knew was the birch tree brooch. I couldn't see his face. The woman took off her hat, took the brooch from his hand and pinned it to the side of the hat, above the brim. Every movement she made had the grace of a wild animal and I knew it could only be some manifestation of Bedwen – here in the mundane surroundings of a busy airport cafeteria!

She put the hat back on and reached out her hand to Tigerface. I froze, afraid of what might happen when their hands touched – but I need not have worried and I chided myself for having fallen for Tigerface's story on the plane. He took her hand, stood up and, hand-in-hand they left the room and disappeared into the crowd.

The girl behind the counter was holding out my coffee and waiting for me to pay but I was far away up on a Welsh hillside with jackdaws flying overhead. The counter-girl said, 'Sir?' to bring me back into reality and I paid for the drink and went to sit down. I was still convinced that there must be a simple explanation until I realised that there could have been no way Bedwen, if it had been her, could have known that we were going to land at Heathrow!

POSTSCRIPT.

I started this story by saying how I had read Tigerface's obituary in the *Telegraph* and realised that I was now free to repeat what he had told me on that memorable flight from Nairobi back in 1962. I had just written the final paragraph and given a copy to a friend to edit, when the postman delivered a letter from Evans, Evans and Evans, Solicitors at Abergavenny, and I experienced a kind of *déjà vu*. The name immediately rang a bell – they were the solicitors who Tigerface's Aunt Becca had used when she was fighting the War Office over possession of her parent's farm. I had thought at the time that the Welsh must be hard up for surnames but I realise now they were all probably related in some way – the solicitors I mean, not the Welsh.

In the past, I would have called this a mere coincidence but, now I am familiar with *Synchronicity,* I would suspect that this phenomena has been involved.

The letter was very brief. It stated that a client of theirs, one David Townsend, a retired photographer, had died recently and they were the executors of his will. As he had no living relations, his money had been left to a charity, but two items were to be passed on to me. Their client had not known my address but had known the name of my publishers and they had tracked me down through these. I should say here that, after leaving the

R.A.F., I had done a variety of jobs and had latterly had some modest success in writing novels.

The solicitors' letter asked if I would contact them and, if not too inconvenient, to call at their offices in Abergavenny.

Conveniently, or perhaps synchronistically, I was due to be in South Wales the following week, so I rang and booked an appointment. I drove down in my camper-van and met a Mr Evans who was far too young to be one of the original Evans' but was a pleasant enough fellow. His office was across the street from the cattle market and I could hear the lowing of cows through his open window. He sat behind a large antique wooden desk that had probably been his grandfather's, and told me that the late David Townsend had left all his money to a charity – The Smile Train – that arranges for children in developing countries to have surgery to repair their faces when they had been born with hare-lips or cleft palates. I could see that this would be a cause close to his late client's heart and said so. Mr Evans agreed.

I asked if David Townsend had been married and he confirmed that he had. He looked at some notes on his desk and told me that in 1962 he had married one Bedwen Jacdo who had died just three weeks before his client. Before I could ask about children, he stated in legal jargonese, that there was 'no issue from the union'. I wondered about the two deaths having been so close together and asked what David Townsend had died from.

Mr Evans took a death certificate out of a file and read out, 'Cause of death – Myocardial Infarction'. He then put the certificate away, leaned back in his leather chair and said, 'My grandfather would have called it a broken heart!'

Just then a young woman came into the office carrying a tray with two cups of tea and four dry biscuits. I was then wondering if Tigerface and Bedwen had wanted children –I was sure that they would have! Perhaps they even prayed for them. Was Daniel M'wangi's God not *All* mighty – or had they forgotten to face Mount Kenya when they prayed?

Mr Evans broke into my idle reverie to tell me that the late David Townsend had left a rather well-worn blanket to me, together with a small sealed packet with the instructions that I was to be asked to return 'the enclosed' to the place where it 'belonged'. Mr Evans added that he would be grateful if I would undertake this request, as there were no other instructions for him should I be unwilling to do so.

The blanket, which was in an open polythene bag was, as I had expected, the one Aunt Becca had given to Tigerface when he had first arrived at the camp and I looked forward to trying out its special qualities. I signed some sort of receipt but I didn't open the smaller packet there and then. However, as soon as I was out of the office, I went into a cafe and broke the seal. The 'enclosed' was, as you may well have guessed, the enamel brooch in the form of a birch tree. I examined it with care and was sure that it was the same one, even though the last time I had held it was on that flight from Africa nearly half a century before.

I was very ready to carry out Tigerface's last wishes but where did the brooch 'belong'? Rather obviously, somewhere in the valley above the old army camp. Probably in the castle that Aunt Becca and Bedwen had called Castell-y-bwlch.

Many times in the years since that flight with Tigerface, I had thought of visiting the valley and finding the castle but I never had. Perhaps I was afraid of discovering that it wasn't really there and the whole story *had* been made up by Tigerface on that flight. But, if that had been so – what about the woman with the violet-coloured eyes who had met him at the airport?

Anyway, now I would *have* to go – I owed him that! One thing I have learned about Synchronicity is that, when you realise that you are caught up in a synchronistic event, you just follow your instincts or feelings and you are somehow guided to the right action or conclusion.

I stopped overnight in my camper van in a lay-by near Abergavenny, risking being moved on in the night by a police patrol, so that I could make an early start to Groesvaen and Castell-y-bwlch in the morning. The weather was not as it had been in Tigerface's Barefoot Summer. There was a cold wind blowing and a threat of rain in the hills. There was going to be no joy in skinny-dipping (as they call it now) in the pool by the bridge and I had been rather looking forward to that. Even now, when I am well into my seventies, 'Hope springs eternal...'

Coming into Groesvaen, which must have been much as it was in 1953, except that the post office and the shop had gone and the village school looked as though it was now a holiday home, I looked for someone to direct me to Talybwlch. The main street through the village was deserted and I knocked on several doors without any response. Then a farmer came along the road on a very old and battered grey Ferguson tractor. The farmer looked even older and more battered than his tractor. There was about four days' stubble on his face, his sideburns reminded me of Englelbert Humperdinck in his heyday and his ragged and buttonless raincoat was tied round his waist with orange binder-twine. I waved him down and the tractor came to a juddering stop.

'Talybwlch?' he replied to my query. 'There's nothing there now!' He looked me up and down, obviously thought I was much older than I am and asked, 'Were you one of them soldiers up at the camp? In the war, like?'

I thought it easier to lie and say, 'Yes,' than try to explain. He told me how to get there and drove off down the street in a cloud of exhaust smoke, with his two black and white sheep-dogs watching me impassively from the link-box on the back of the tractor.

I found the track leading up to where the farm, and later the Army Camp had been. I parked the camper-van at the top of the grass-grown track in the place where, during the war, three-ton Bedford lorries would have turned round after delivering supplies and dropping off trainees. I got out of the van and looked about, trying to visualise how it would have been when Tigerface was there. I knew from what he had told me that the camp had been demolished and I had wondered if a new farmhouse might have been built in its place but the farmer on the tractor had been right. Where the main camp must have been all that was there now was a smooth grass field being grazed by a few grubby-looking sheep. Near to where I was standing was the flat concrete base of the demolished Guardroom and, in the centre of the field, was something that I thought might be a small standing stone though I was sure that Tigerface would have told me if there had been one within the camp.

Puzzled by this, I walked across the grass to look at it. The sheep scattered as I got near and I could see that it wasn't a stone at all but a three-bay urinal, standing forlornly in the centre of the field that had once been an army camp. The JCB operator who Tigerface had seen must have had a sense of humour similar to mine, and had carefully demolished the ablutions block around it and left the urinal standing as a kind of bizarre monument.

I was tempted to use it but the sheep had stopped grazing and were watching me and I felt stupidly embarrassed and walked back to the van to collect the brooch and take it up to the castle. I locked the van, walked up the track and was climbing over the stile when I realised that I had left my wet-weather gear in the van. Against all the rules of walking in the hills, I decided to carry on without it, even though the wind had strengthened and the air was decidedly cold. I could recognise the shape of the valley as being how Tigerface had described it but there were no pine trees and certainly no birches, just a scattering of stunted hawthorns.

I thought of taking off my shoes to see if I could experience the transformation that Tigerface had experienced but it was too cold and, now I was here, I was increasingly sceptical about the more mystical aspects of his story. I came to the bridge and the pool but the surface was rippled by the wind and was not inviting and, as I crossed the bridge, I thought I heard a distant rumble of thunder. I hurried on up the track to the castle – but it wasn't there!

Where Tigerface had described it, standing in the gap in the ridge, was just a huge pile of moss-covered stones which might once have been a castle but bore little resemblance to one now.

During that flight from Nairobi he had described it to me in two different ways. In the first, when he and

Bedwen had found the jackdaw's hoard, the castle had been complete, if practically deserted. When he went back later, after his Aunt Becca had died, it had been derelict and neglected but still standing. Could it have collapsed to this state in the fifty or so years since then? I thought not and in my mind nearly wrote off the whole of Tigerface's story as a clever fiction.

But I still had the brooch and had promised Mr Evans that I would return 'the enclosed' to the place where it 'belonged'. Might there be a place in the pile of stones where I could conceal it in such a way that it would not be found and carried away by an inquisitive hiker?

I clambered to the top of the heap and from there I could see into the next valley. A storm was rolling up towards me with lightning flashing amongst the black clouds and I could smell the rain on the wind. I did not have long to find a hiding place for the brooch if I was going to have any chance of getting back to the van before the storm overwhelmed me. The topmost stone of the pile had the rusty stump of an iron post protruding from the centre and I grasped this to haul myself up. Was this all that was left of the beacon that was there when Tigerface sat on the roof with Bedwen? I could see that it had been set in a hole in the stone and that molten lead had been poured around the base to secure it, which seemed to confirm this. Holding the post with one hand to steady myself against the rising wind, I took the brooch from my pocket, meaning to slip it down a deep crevice where it would not be found again.

There was a crack of thunder and I realised that holding an iron post on top of a huge pile of stones was not the most sensible thing to be doing and let go of the post and dropped to my knees to crawl away. There was a momentary pause in the storm, the brooch dropped from my hand on to the stone slab, and a jackdaw flew in from the direction of one of the cliffs and perched on the iron post. It cocked its head to one side, gave me a look similar to the one the woman in the green dress had given me all those years ago at Heathrow, which this time I interpreted as a 'thank you', picked up the brooch in its beak and flew back towards the cliff. I felt a curious kind of a reverse *déjà vu* and wondered if some new cycle of events had been started. I did not think about this for long! I dropped off the big slab, scrambled down the pile of stones and went as fast as I could back down the track.

When one is in one's seventies, running is out of the question and the storm overtook me as I crossed the bridge by the pool. When I reached the van, I was soaked to the skin, shivering violently and my teeth were chattering like an old-fashioned typewriter. I stripped off, put on dry pyjamas, made a cup of tea with shaking hands, spread the 'magic' blanket, sunny-side up, on the bed and wriggled underneath it. A subtle scent of honeysuckle filled the van and the blanket warmed me through in a very short time.

If I told you that, when I woke up a few hours later, it was dark, the storm had passed and, as I opened the van door and stepped barefoot onto the wet grass in the moonlight, I heard someone playing Lilli Marlene on a mouth organ, I would not expect you to believe me.

THE PRAT ON THE BEACH

THE PRAT ON THE BEACH
The Gower Coast, South Wales.

Joyce turned on her back and looked up at the blueness of the sky, then trod water and looked back at the beach. Gerald, her brother, was walking along the tideline, his cassock black against the gleaming white of the dunes. She was cross with him, the elder brother who she had adored as a child.

When they had been much younger they had played in those dunes, hiding and leaping out at one another in showers of sand before swimming together in the clear sea. Then he had had his 'call' and gone all religious. Even today, after three days of sunshine and with the sea as warm as she had ever known it, he wouldn't come in to swim with her. He had studied the horizon as she undressed behind him and put on her new bikini.

'For God's sake, Gerry,' she had urged him. 'There's no one else about, I am your sister and surely even priests wear underpants. You can swim in those.'

But he had shaken his head. 'I'll wait for you. Don't go out too far.'

She *was* out too far, she knew that but then she was the captain of her college swimming team and could swim for miles if she had to. Even though Gerald was her brother he was a prat, swallowing all that religious nonsense. He wouldn't even read the Richard Dawkins' books which had proved conclusively to her that God was unnecessary nowadays. Everything was decided by your genes, so-called spiritual matters were all in the imagination and Mankind no longer needed to invent a God for themselves.

She swam even farther out just to tease, then lay floating on her back again watching the small clouds drift across the blue dome above. With slight movements of her hands and legs she could float indefinitely.

The small white clouds were getting bigger, some had grey patches and, when she looked seawards, there were towering clouds, one of which had a top that spread out like a giant hammer. Lightning flickered and flashed silently in the dark, lower part of the cloud just above the horizon. The surface of the sea, so flat and calm a few minutes ago was rippled and a cold breeze cooled and tickled her face. Don't panic, she told herself and turned to swim for the shore. The dunes and her brother's tiny figure now seemed very far away.

She had hardly done a dozen strokes when the wind struck hard, the ripples turned to wavelets, which soon formed into larger waves which sometimes hid the land from sight, the wind edging the wave-tops with white foam before whipping it away in a cold and painful spray. She felt terribly alone and vulnerable, searching with her eyes along the dunes for a sight of Gerald, though hoping that he had had the sense to run up to the village and phone the coastguards.

She caught a glimpse of a figure in black clothes. It must be Gerald, still on the beach, though he appeared much shorter than he had looked before. It was at this moment that the cramps caught her, stabbing at her belly and stiffening her left leg in exquisite agony as had happened a month or so before in the college pool. Then the lifeguard had helped her out of the water. There was no lifeguard here, there never was on this little-used beach. She was going to die, to drown here with just that prat of a brother on the beach to tell their parents of her stupidity in swimming out so far. She tried to float on her back but the pain in her guts kept her doubled up and she swallowed a mouthful of water, salt, bitter and cold.

A black fin appeared on her right and another on her left. Sharks!

Now she panicked, striking out wildly towards the shore, dragging her stiff leg and trying to ignore the pain tearing at her guts. The fins were nearer now, moving into position, one close in to her side of her and she saw the grinning face of a dolphin break the surface. Not sharks, thank God!

Now there was a dolphin tight in to either side of her and she reached out an arm to hold round the smooth black rubbery fins on the dolphin's backs. A feeling of love, care and security enveloped her as the two bore her easily through the waves towards the beach. The pains in her guts and leg were replaced by dull aches as they reached the breakers.

Gerald was there, standing in the waves up to his chest, holding out his arms to make a cradle to take her from the dolphins. He waded ashore, carrying the limp body of his sister and laid her on the sand above the high water mark in a place where a marram-topped dune cut the force of the wind. Joyce opened her eyes, looked up and saw him standing above her, his wet cassock clinging to his body and she could hear his teeth chattering over the whistle of the wind in the coarse grass. She was angry again.

'Why didn't you go and phone the coast-guards? I could have drowned out there!'

'There wasn't time. I knelt on the beach and prayed.'

'God, you're a prat,' she told him. 'If it hadn't been for those two dolphins...'

Father Gerald crouched awkwardly and picked her up in his arms again. 'We must get you somewhere warm.'

THE FERRYMAN'S DAUGHTER

THE FERRYMAN'S DAUGHTER

It was nearly two and twenty years ago when I first rode down the track into the little fishing village. I could see a cluster of folk at the unenclosed burial ground beyond the houses where a body was being lowered into a grave. It seemed that all the villagers were present at the graveside as the single street was empty of people and the beach was likewise deserted. No boats were visible on the calm sea though I counted thirty skin-covered round coraghs and one double-ended wooden boat drawn up on the shingle. Beyond these, a recent wreck lay awkwardly on its side. Cleansed of all it contained, no doubt, but the hulk was untouched, obviously not granted to any person by the King, who in custom, tradition and law, owns all such wrecks.

I reined-in well back from the silent group of mourners, sat astride Jonquil and counted the villagers. There were three score men and about the same number of women. A host of children hung about, some crying though the adults were stoic, as I would have expected. Death is an inevitable end to life.

From where I sat, unnoticed as yet, I identified as the dead man's widow the woman who was the first to cast the God-speed soil into the open grave. She was in her forties and stood tall and straight with a plait of fair hair down her back in the custom of the Uplanders. The other women wore theirs cut short and fringed over the eyes in the style of womenfolk of the coast and the Lower Lands.

I had travelled far that day along the cliffs and beaches of this barren and dangerous coast to count the people and to assess the tax value of the village for the King. His woodstock emblem on my surcoat ensured my safe passage; there was not a bandit nor cutpurse in the kingdom who would dare offend a man thus emblazoned and my wolf-hound, Wraith, kept the beggers at a convenient distance though I would sometimes toss a coin or two to the most deserving.

The woman with the plait turned and left the graveside as the men filled in the pit and I besat Jonquil watching her as she entered a building with a bedraggled bush hanging over the door. It was without doubt an inn and alehouse, though few travellers were likely on this lonely coastal track.

Without dismounting, I assessed the village tax *by view* as one hundred silver marks per year, based on the apparent wealth - or lack of it. If there had been some sign of a dwelling for a person of any nobility I would have made it one hundred and fifty marks. But no such dwelling was visible, though there was a splendid site for a comfortable manor house on a ridge behind and above the village.

I rode Jonquil forward slowly as the children, spotting a stranger, rushed towards me, then hung back on seeing the woodstock blazon on my chest and hearing Wraith's low growl of warning.

The children formed into untidy ranks on either side of us as I rode towards the inn along the dusty street. Many were poorly dressed but the most striking thing about them was that more than half of the hundred or so brats looked as though they were all of the same breeding. I had known this before in other small and isolated communities.

The woman with the plait came out of the door below the hanging bush and came forward to take Jonquil's bridle. She had a twist of black cloth around her upper arm but was not otherwise apparently in mourning. She turned towards me and spoke.

On seeing her face, it was hard to maintain a gentlemanly composure. Her ears stuck out like the handles on a quart tankard and one eye, a brown one, was seemingly studying Jonquil's right hoof whilst the other, as blue as the sky above, appeared to be following the flight of the gulls over the rooftops.

'I beg your pardon,' I said, 'I was distracted by a soreness from the saddle. Repeat yourself, if you would be so good.'

'I was asking the gentleman if he wished to stay here tonight. It is a humble place - but clean, Sir.'

There was no other building of any consequence in the village and I unhorsed and followed as she led Jonquil to a well-swept and seemingly little-used stable at the rear. The oats were wholesome and the straw smelt fresh. A boy, who called the woman 'Aunt', took Jonquil's trappings to be cleaned and polished. I gave him a halfpenny coin, which he took eagerly and turned over in his hand as though he saw few of these. Another such coin was promised if Jonquil was rubbed down that night and groomed to my satisfaction for the morning.

The room to which I was shown was as clean and as pleasant for me as the stable had been for Jonquil. I stripped and washed in the cold water I found ready in a clay pot, redressed myself in fresh clothes and left Wraith guarding my baggage, then went along to the messing room at the end of the passage. A jorum of ale stood on the scrubbed wooden table and I sat and drank from this as the woman busied herself at the fireplace stirring a cookpot from which the smell of fish and herbs drifted around the room. The fire burned with a low but intense blue flame. Stormwood most likely, collected from the beach.

'Good woman,' I called to her. 'What is your name?'

She turned and came across to me, ladle in hand. Her brown eye was examining my boots under the table whilst the blue one watched for spiders over my head.

'If I ever had a name,' she said, 'it is long forgotten. I am known to all as the Ferryman's Daughter.'

'The burying?' I ventured. 'Your husband?'

'To all intentions, Jack was that. But when the friars ever came by there was no silver in the pot - and weddings are not done for coppers. Jack Ladd was my man and none here argued with that.'

The name was familiar to me, from tavern-talk only a few weeks before when I had been doing the King's assessment in the Upper Lands. But *that* Jack Ladd had been dead many years.

'How did he die?' I asked.

'Over-excitement in bed,' she replied with a wry look, and turned back towards the cookpot.

'There was a Jack Ladd in the Upper Lands once,' I called after her. 'His name became a byword there for lustiness and daring.'

There was an ancient hatred between the Lords of the Upper and the Lower Lands and few people ventured the difficult mountain passes between the two.

'That could have been *my* Jack,' she called back to me. 'He lived there once - as I did too.'

'You're not the Ferryman's Daughter from Rhydycastell?' I asked as she brought a dish of fish soup to the table.

'I may be - and I may be not,' she replied. 'Now that Jack is gone I may be once again.'

'Will you sup at the table with me?' I asked.

'No, Sir. That would not be right,' she replied studying the floor and the underside of the stone roof tiles at the same time.

'There is none to speak ill if *I* don't,' I said. 'Unless others are expected.'

'There will only be yourself,' she replied. 'Few travel this way.'

Even though I thought it unmannerly to question her further, my curiosity prompted me to ask, 'You have no children, then?'

'The Good Lord in his wisdom denied me that,' she replied without discomfiture. 'But I am 'Aunt' to most of the younglings hereabouts. That will have to do for me.'

'Sup with me,' I asked again. I nosed a story here and the evening would be long.

'As you wish, Sir,' the Ferryman's Daughter replied and fetched her own bowl from the fireside.

The soup was good if one ignored the fishes' heads whose blind eyes stared as wildly askance as mine host's. The bread was soft and free of grit; the miller's stones must be of sound rock.

She supped graciously enough not to offend, then brought a bowl of apples to the table and sat in silence as I ate mine. It seemed that starting questions would be needed, if I were to draw out the tale I sensed was there.

'Was it your Jack Ladd who entered Castell-Carreg-Afon by the turdeshoot, some twenty years ago?'

The brown eye opposite registered surprise that I should know of such an incident, whilst the blue one indicated a degree of pride. I have never seen such an expression before and I bit deep into the apple to hide my amusement.

'It was he,' she answered simply and I waited hoping for more. I was not to be disappointed.

'My father was the ferryman at Rhydycastell before I was born, Sir. Do you know the place?'

I knew it well enough. Castell-Carreg-Afon, the castle of the river rock, stood on a crag near the ford a short mile above the point where the torrent swept into the Dragon's Maw; a gorge so hazardous that no boat had ever survived the passage. Few men had attempted it and no boat carried there by fate was known to have emerged with a living crew.

The ford by the castle was passable by a horseman and, in time of drought by oxen carts, but the usual passage was by a ferryboat rowed by a strong and skilful river-man. I had heard that for many years there had been a woman at the oars. A woman with unusual eyes!

'I know the place well, daughter of the ferryman,' I said. 'I dined with the Lord of the Upper Lands last autumn. Will you take ale with me?'

There is nothing like a sufficiency of ale to loosen tongues and this woman was no exception. It needed only a little questioning to launch her into her story; and my position has given me some modest skills at this questioning game.

The Ferryman's Daughter drew up a comfortable seat for me on one side of the fire that hissed and crackled as she settled herself in a high-backed chair across the hearth.

'My Jack would never let I sit here,' she said. 'This was his chair.'

'When did he die?' I asked. Then I must have looked uncomfortable remembering that she had said he had died of overexcitement in bed. She saw my discomfiture and laughed.

'It was three days back and it wasn't here. Jack was inclined to share his favours around the village.'

'You seem to be taking the loss of your... your Jack well,' I remarked, wishing that I had started with another subject.

'We understood each other,' she said calmly, her one eye examining my stockinged feet stretched out towards the fire, while her other eye followed the smoke as it was drawn up the chimney. A frosty night makes a fire draw well.

'Have you ever seen the salmon run in the autumn spate, Sir?' she asked.

'They were running when I was at Rhydycastell last year,' I told her. 'They were hustling upstream in their thousands, leaping at every little fall. Lord Cedric and I dined on salmon at the castle. A delicate fish though I fear my Lord over-ate of it.'

'God damn Cedric the Greedy,' she exclaimed with a cold personal malice in her voice.

'Steady,' I cautioned, not wishing her tongue to put her in danger, then, realising that Lord Cedric held no sway in the Lower Lands, I let it pass. There was a tale here that I wished to know.

'My Jack with women was like the salmon in the sea. Finding a river he had to run up it to spawn. My Jack was a good spawner. Did you see him in the village children?'

I had never seen Jack himself but I could picture him as the father of most of the children who had met me when I had arrived. Were there no other fecund men in the village? A tale indeed! I sat back and supped the ale, waiting for her to continue.

'Each woman was a challenge to him. Always one for a challenge, my Jack. When he was a lad one had only to say 'I dare you...' and he was off to do whatever had been suggested. He climbed the Darren for the raven's eggs, dived off Carreg Fawr into the river, put nettles under the tail of the priest's horse. Oh, he was a one,' she sighed. 'And I'll miss him.'

I waited, knowing now that the silence would lead her to continue. She leaned forward and tossed a sea-whitened log onto the fire.

'I loved that man since I was a lass,' she said. 'But he could have his pick of all the girls in the Upper Lands and never gave me more than a glance; what with my funny eyes and these.' She flicked at her ears with her hands, grimaced and drank again from her tankard.

'He'd get me to row him over the river, promising the penny fare but he'd leap ashore and run off laughing.

I'd pretend to be cross but, in truth, Sir, it was the only time I had him to myself and I'd row him back later, knowing he would cheat me of my penny once again.'

I waited once more. A silence can often bring forth a tale that a question might frighten away.

'One day he heard that Lord Cedric's daughter, Elinor *Bach*, was bathing in the river and he went upstream and swam down under the water to rise beside her as naked as she was. Her maid, who was on the bank, squealed like a stuck pig when she saw Jack pop up like a giant otter, which was unfortunate as Lord Cedric was riding back from his hawking and heard her squeals. He rode over and saw Jack and Elinor *Bach* as they climbed out of the water; Jack holding her hand to help her up the bank for she was a small woman, though well formed. Lord Cedric struck Jack about the body with his riding whip, had his servants throw him in the river and vowed to hang him if he ever came near his daughter again.'

'And did he?' I asked, too eager to restrain myself.

'He did, Sir, but only the one time. He could be a fool, my Jack. He had got it into his head that Elinor *Bach* would welcome a visit from him and he worked out a plan. One night he stole the ropes his father, the miller, used for hauling up sacks of grain.

My ears were by now sticking out like those of the woman opposite. I could hardly wait for what was to come. The way she spoke the word '*Bach*' intrigued me. As plain Bach it means little or dear, even little *and* dear

124

and I have no doubt this is what Elinor's parents and wet-nurse would have called her as a child. The Ferryman's Daughter said it with a subtly different accent- *Bach* - which implies small and useless.

'As I have said, Sir, my Jack was a strong young man, skilled in the climbing of rock and he knew the chamber in the castle where Elinor *Bach* slept. Can you recall the shape of Castell Carreg Afon, Sir? There is a tower above the river with a drop down to the water below.

'That rock is sheer,' I replied. It has always been a fascination to me to study castles for their weaknesses. In troubled times such knowledge may have a value. 'There was *no* way up there.'

'That's true, Sir, but a little way around the bluff the rock is creviced from water level to the outfall of the turdeshoot. The river carries away the night soil from the castle. I have no doubt that there are bars on the turdeshoot *now*.

'So it was true...?'

'He did that, Sir. It was the only way he could think of to pass the guards. That castle has never been taken and probably never will be.'

I had heard of a castle in France being infiltrated and taken by soldiers climbing in that way, though it would be a task worthy of great reward. I don't think I could have done that, even for ten thousand marks of silver. I've noticed that the jackdaws avoid the nearness of a turdeshoot when seeking nest-holes.

I moved my foot to push a log further onto the fire and wondered as I did it if this action might offend. It is said that you have to know a friend for three years before you can poke their fire without risking offence - but none was taken here. The Ferryman's Daughter saw my hesitation and nodded assent so I shoved the end of the log well into the flaming centre of the fire. A cascade of sparks flew upward and glowing rings crawled around and devoured each other on the soot-caked stonework behind the flames.

'Jack planned it all out. He chose a night when the moon would rise at midnight and persuaded me, as big a fool as he, to row him across in the darkness and wait in the place where the rock overhangs, my boat tied to a little alder bush growing in a crack of the rock.'

There was something I needed to be clear about, to see the whole picture.

'Your father, the ferryman, where was his part in all this?'

'He was long dead, Sir, as was my mother. That's how the ferryboat came to me. I had no other way to earn my living - no man wanted the likes of me.' She grimaced again and added, 'Except when the river was to be crossed.'

'I see,' I said simply and motioned to her to continue.

'I rowed Jack across in the dark, knowing the river well, put him safe on a ledge with the coil of rope around his shoulders and drifted back beneath the overhang where I tied fast to wait. Now, Sir, I must tell it you as Jack told me.'

I knew that the continuance of the story was safe and excused myself to the privy house, looking in on my hound, Wraith, before returning. He was lying on the bed as I had taught him, warming it for me. His tail swished the coverlet when he heard me enter the room.

Back in the messing-room again I made up the fire whilst the Ferryman's Daughter poured another tankard.

'This one is my gift, Sir,' she said but I had to refuse. It is dangerous when on the King's business, to accept any favours, however small. Tax assessors have lost their heads that way.

She realised the situation and took no offence. For an innkeeper she had a delicate sensibility that I warmed to. This was no ordinary woman and I longed to hear her story through. I took out my purse of small coins and laid it on the stool at my side as a gesture of payment to come. My poke of gold and silver was safe hanging on my belt within my breeks.

'You had just put Jack ashore,' I reminded her gently.

'You wouldn't call it a shore exactly. Just a ledge above the water where Jack waited until the moon rose over the hill. Then he put on one of his father's long dust-coats over his own clothes and started to climb. I could see none of this but as Jack told me it was a moderate scramble, nothing when set against the climb up for the raven's eggs when he were younger. But the moonlight made it all seem unreal and, with the guards on the battlements, he had to be very quiet.

'Well, he reached the turdeshoot and nearly turned back. The rocks below were all splattered and stinking and the stench was awful. If it had only been me who had known his scheme he might have given up but he had boasted to his friends of what he planned and that meant he had to see it through. Stinking turds or no.

'I've only once looked down a turdeshoot, Sir, and from my memory it is a little enough passage. Smaller than a chimney near the stack.'

I had *often* in my travels looked down these places and she was right, Jack must have been a small man to wriggle up such a flue.

'He told me that he tried to hold his breath as he climbed, but that as the passage got smaller he had to wriggle with his shoulders and search with the toes of his buskins for holds and one needs a plentiful breath for doing that. He was hoping that those in the castle were all abed and the guards had relieved themselves earlier. I think, Sir, that I need not add to the telling in detail. You are a man who can picture for himself what it would have been like.'

I imagined the man pushing out the wooden seat and clambering into the garderobe covered from head to foot and stinking to the heavens above. 'I have that picture in my head,' I replied, 'though thankfully not in my nostrils.'

The Ferryman's Daughter laughed.

'Jack told me that he took off his father's much soiled dust-coat and dropped it back down the hole before trying to wash himself with the water in the buckets kept in the garderobe. But he said that he could not do this well and he was afeared that the guards would scent him like rabbits scent a foulmart as he followed dark passages towards where he believed Elinor *Bach*'s room to be. There were rats in the passages, he said, but he had no fear of them. Somehow he found the stairs up to her room and knocked on the door. "It is I, Jack Ladd, come to visit a fair lady," he called through the door and she opened it in her nightwear with a shawl around her shoulders. There was a candle by her bed and he thought that she had not been asleep, though she could not have known that he was coming that night.

'I often picture her opening that door. There stood my Jack, with that silly grin of his, still smeared with turds and with a rope around his shoulders, waiting to be asked in by my fine lady Elinor. Her smelling of lavender, I have no doubt, and him smelling of you-know-what.'

She laughed again and I wanted to know her real name. She deserved to have a name other than the

Ferryman's Daughter. But now was not the time. I smiled an encouragement to continue.

'Jack never told me what he planned to do. Did he hope to bed her? Was the rope to lower her out of the window? Had he thought beyond his getting there? I suspect not! She tried to push the door shut in his face and he stopped this with his leg. She screamed for her father and the guards to come, and Jack had to push into the room and lock the door.

All this while she screamed as though Jack was forcing himself on her - but that was not his way. You recall my saying that the bedchamber was above a sheer drop into the river - that the miller's rope was for Jack to slide down after his visit?'

I nodded, imagining the hubbub in the castle; the guards being called out and stumbling up the narrow stairs with my Lord Cedric shouting orders from below.

'Elinor *Bach* was still screaming rape and murder and Jack told her to be silent or he'd throw her out of the window. "You wouldn't dare," she said and that was the wrong thing to say to Jack Ladd, though whether he intended to, or just to threaten, he never admitted. He took the silly woman up in his arms and lifted her onto the cill, then held her through the open casement, with her screaming like a dying pig all the while. I could hear it from my boat below. Then, because his buskins were slimy with the turds from the climb, he slipped and the two of them tumbled from the window a hundred feet into the river. Elinor *Bach* fell clear but Jack twice hit rock on the way down. I had the boat free in an instant - there is a special knot we use, Sir, and was able to reach them before they were in real danger. Elinor climbed aboard, spluttering about rape and murder so I threatened to hit her with the oar if she did not silence herself while I got my Jack aboard.

'He was nearly drowning which surprised me then as I knew him to be strong swimmer but with a broken hip-bone, as we later found he had, no man can stay afloat for long. Elinor *Bach,* in her sodden nightwear sat on the stern seat as I pulled Jack into the boat and all the time the current was taking us down towards the Dragon's Maw. I had to row, Sir, harder than I had ever had to row before. Up river I rowed, afeared of arrows from above so I got Elinor *Bach* to call up to the guards not to shoot. This she did readily enough, Sir, what with her being in the boat but it was still quite dark though the cocks across the river were calling for the sun.

'I took her to the landing and put her ashore on the Castle side. I thought of asking for the penny fare but I had not rowed her across the river, and she was still in her nightwear and shivering like an aspen leaf in a summer breeze. Elinor *Bach* is known for having no fondness for jokes at her expense so I held my tongue and pushed away from the jetty. She stood there in the dim-dawn cursing Jack and myself and saying that her father would hang us both. Above us I could see the castle gallows against the fading moon and was cold-scared to my heart, Sir. Jack, meanwhile, was lying in the boat groaning and not sitting up so I knew he was hurt sore and bad.

'I rested on the oars and floated slow, drifting in towards the castle rock then, fearing arrows, pulled in beneath the overhang and tiedup to the alder bush with a slip-knot as before to think out a plan.

'I had no doubt that Lord Cedric would hang my Jack as he would a troublesome dog though I doubted if he would hang me as I had saved his daughter's life that night. I would lose my boat and my work though, of that I was sure and a whore's life in a distant town held little appeal. There was only one course out. Better to die with Jack, I thought and eased him into the slight protection of the stern seat, him groaning with each movement.

'The roar from the rapids of the Dragon's Maw seemed suddenly loud in my ears as I pulled at the slip knot and rowed downstream. It was lighter now and archers lined the battlements above - dark heads against the dawn. Lord Cedric's voice shouted, 'Shoot to kill. Shoot the rapist - and the Ferryman's Daughter. Shoot. A silver mark for a successful shot.'

'Arrows hissed around my head and splashed into the water, but not one hit the boat. I believe that Elinor *Bach* was less highly thought of by the archer-men than my Jack was. It was likely too that the soldiers knew I was in the boat, and most of them knew me as I had often ferried them over the river to the village tavern of an evening. I was glad now that I had not insisted on the fares when they returned spent-out at midnights. Commonly I had rowed them over for free in time to sober up for morning-muster. And that day I forgave them for their cruel jokes about my eyes and ears.

'But it was leap from the pot and drop into the fire for Jack and me, so to speak. Out of arrow-shot I was into the snatch and tug of the current. I pulled on the one oar to turn the bows upstream and enter the gorge stern first, the better to see the dangers and my heart went cold inside of me once more. The light was gathering its strength and the cliffs were rearing ahead of us like frightened horses. The roar from the gorge deepened and I could almost believe that a dragon dwelt there ready to devour us, boat and all. But the gap between the walls was dark and I knew that in the darkness I would have no chance to steer clear of the rocks in the river's-bed itself. I prayed then, Sir, as I had never prayed before but rowed as I prayed, working to keep the bows upstream towards the current, for the Lord helps those who help themselves my father, the ferryman, used to say.

'Then, the Good Lord having heard my prayer, the sun peeped over the hill and its light shot into the gorge like a flaming lance, lighting the barren heights above and glistening on the wet walls below. A rainbow in the spray gave me hope and I guided the boat stern-first down the first long tongue of water, watching for the eddies and the humps that rocks make when they are hidden just below the surface. Though I had never been near the Dragon's Maw before, I had often rowed passengers across the river when there was spate from mountain rains and I knew the dangers and the signs of such rocks, Sir.

'Into the gorge we went, me tense at the oars, my Jack lying groaning in the bilge water that slopped from side to side as I steered to left or right. I had no time to see him comfortable; one misjudgement, one clumsy stroke and the boat would have been smashed on a rock or into the wall. Twice the stern dipped deep into the white water that stops a tongue-tip and after the second time the boat was half-full. Jack was trying to keep his head above the water but he was clearly hurt badly and lacking in strength for the task. The rush of the water had slowed now and we drifted between high walls, me searching for a ledge or some snag to tie to but the walls were sheer and were polished as smooth as Lord Cedric's riding gaiters. Then, in the gloom ahead I saw a little beach of pebbles and I ran at it, the boat sluggish as a rotten log.

'When the bow touched stone I pulled my sodden skirts up to my waist and leapt ashore holding the mooring rope to draw the boat onto the stones. Jack was floating and bumped against the seat. He screamed then and that scream of his pain echoed up into the gorge above and was increased a hundred-fold like the devils howling in the heat of Hell. He screamed again when I pulled him forward and laid him over the centre seat, but I had to do it, Sir, or he'd have drowned within the boat.

'In the bows I kept a leather bucket, tied with a cord as my father had shown me, not just in case it was to fall overboard but to stop drunken soldiers stealing it; they are a light-fingered lot and a sound bucket is worth a quart of ale at any inn - with no questions asked.'

The Ferryman's Daughter looked exhausted. She was telling her story well for I had been *with* her in the boat on that dreadful journey and was anxious to know how she had won to safety – as she surely had, or we would not be sitting together that night.

She stood and swung an iron pot of water round so that it hung over the hot coals.

'Shall I make up the fire?' I asked.

'No, Sir. My tale is nearly done. Perhaps you have heard enough and wish for your bed.'

'I will not sleep until I have heard it through,' I replied. 'You had mentioned a leather bucket – tied with a cord.'

The Ferryman's Daughter sat and pulled her skirts around her legs. I was uncomfortable about this business of her not having a name; she must have had one once. I asked, 'Most boats are given names, what did you call yours?'

'Boat,' she replied simply and it seemed that names might not be as important to her as to others. Still it worried away at the back of my mind though she had started her story again.

'I used the bucket to bale the water from the boat while Jack hung over the seat still groaning. His clothes, like mine, were heavy with water and a cold draught blew through the chasm, which here was as wide as a village street. I could not stay there in the chill or my Jack and myself would have died of hunger or, more likely, congestion of the lungs. Yet downstream I could hear more roaring water where the cliffs came close together once more. A fish leapt in the stream and dark fins appeared and disappeared in the current. At the water's edge I could see the salmon swimming upstream, dark shapes in the dark water. Thousands upon thousands - swimming up to spawn, though many would end their days in skillets or in the bellies of otters. It's a powerful urge that would drive them up that awful stream. In a way they were a comfort to me; to know some other living things had passed though the place where shortly Jack and Boat and I were to venture.'

I noted that it was now 'Boat' rather than 'the boat' and wondered if my question on names had been responsible for this, but the Ferryman's Daughter was now telling how she had thought to use the miller's rope that was still around Jack Ladd's shoulders to tie the oars in the same way as the bucket had been tied.

'The Good Lord had given me the strength to hold them tight all through the upper reaches for, if I had lost an oar, the river would have taken us for sure. Now I had the chance to make them safe for I was tiring, Sir. It had been a full day and a night with no sleep and little food. With the free end of the rope I tied my Jack to the seat. I would not want to find that I had survived if he had been washed away into the river. When I launched into the stream, the backs of the salmon were showing all around me but those innocent fishes were heading the other way to where Lord Cedric's men would do doubt be waiting for them with gaffs, spears and nets.

'For a while I lay forward on the oars floating down what must have a very deep section for they say, and I know it to be true, that slow waters run deeply. I listened to the roaring ahead, trying to assess the dangers and praying for strength of arm. Then the water started to flow faster and darker and Boat pitched from side to side as we rounded the bend that hid the view ahead. The gorge closed to a gap that it would be too narrow for an oxcart to pass and the water poured through, then rose in a wave so that, contrary to nature, as we rode over we were travelling uphill to the top. I had no chance to use the oars; there was not the width between the walls of wet black rock so I drew them inboard and held tight to the seat either side of me. Up and over that great hump we went and down the other side like children on a snow-sledge. A shout was drawn from me as we careered down, though I cannot recall if it was a shout of fear or a shout of joy, for before me I could see the chasm widen and far beyond lay an expanse of blue water that I knew must be the sea, though I had never seen it before, being of the Upper Lands beyond the mountains.'

Warm and comfortable in dry clothes and basking in the heat from a mountain of glowing coals I tried to imagine Boat, dwarfed by those giant crags and admired the courage of this woman who had risked everything to save her man from the noose. There was a nobleness and generosity of spirit in her that one seldom finds even in those more highly born. She deserved to have a name.

'I trust I am not boring you, Sir,' she said, having evidently noticed my abstraction.

'Dear God - no,' I replied. 'I cannot recall an evening where I have been entertained in so worthwhile a manner. Please do continue.'

'The gorge-mouth opened to the sea and the lower rocks were green and brown with hanging weeds. Creatures that I now know to be periwinkles and limpets, clung to the rocks and the water, though not rough, heaved up and down again in a manner I did not know then, coming from a land of rivers and mountains. I had heard that the sea was full of salt so I dipped a finger and tasted it and found this to be true. It was the taste of life and safety and freedom for I knew that Lord Cedric's arm could not reach my Jack and me here.

'There were few easy places to land there on the rocks and with Jack in such a state I had to get him to where others could carry him ashore so I rowed east along the coast until I saw the smoke from the chimneys of this village and came ashore here, Sir.'

She stopped as though that would be all I would want to know and peered into the hot water pot.

'How badly hurt was your Jack?' I asked.

'The bone of his hip was broken. Some of the men of the village carried him up the beach on a door from a net-hut and took him to this inn. The people of the village were kind to us then, Sir, but it took many months of nursing before my Jack could walk again. Even then the bones must have set crooked for there was no physician here, and forever-after Jack walked somewhat sideways like the crabs in the shallows by the beach. He would never go in a boat again neither, Sir. He said that he had had enough of boats for a lifetime and a half, which was a pity for Boat was better for the fishing than those round, skin-covered coraghs the fishermen use hereabouts.

'How did you earn a living for yourselves?' I asked.

'I hired Boat to any man whose coragh needed repair. Jack was good at the mending of their coraghs and and their nets and was happy to stay on the land busy with his net needle while I rowed the fisherman out to where the codfish were feeding. We earned enough to repay the debt to the innkeeper, for we lived then in a hut by the beach, which we had built from storm-wood and stones, with a roof of turf. We had no children of our own, Sir, with me being barren and, with plenty of fish for free, we had a sufficiency. Much later we were left this place by the Inn-keeper who was also childless and for whom I had been able to do a kindness or two after his wife had died.'

'How did Jack settle down to a quiet life?' I asked, recalling the story she had just told and the tales of his exploits as a youth that I had heard in the Upper Lands.

'At first he fretted badly, Sir, being unable to walk about much but then he found a new interest when the menfolk were out fishing.'

I guessed at her meaning and this would have explained all the looking-alikeness of the children I had seen that day, the ones who had called her 'Aunt', for a broken hip does not destroy a man's fertility as some other injuries might. She told me this with no suggestion of complaint or aggrievance such as most women would have shown.

I smiled across the hearth at her and there was a twinkle in her blue eye and a knowing look in the brown one.

'You were not unhappy about that, then?' I asked, feeling that my question was only just on the acceptable side of rudeness.

'It can get boring in a boat when the cod-fish are not biting,' she said. 'And unless you are a mating salmon, a run up a barren river can do no harm.'

I laughed out loud and she laughed with me. I had not been so at ease with a woman since my Elizabeth had died of the black flux soon after we had been married so long past.

'You *must* have had a name,' I said and she went silent.

Eventually she spoke. 'Since you asked me that earlier, Sir, I have worried at it like a puppy at a leather slipper. I believe my mother, God rest her soul, called me Kate.'

'Then your name would have been Katherine,' I told her.

'Oh no, Sir, only Kate - a simple name for a simple person. I was never called Katherine.'

I stood up. 'Well, Kate,' I said. 'I am for my bed. I thank you for your story.'I bowed to her as to a lady, though why I did so did not strike me as odd at the time.

My hound, Wraith, yawned and stretched himself on the bed when I entered the bed-chamber carrying a candlestick from the messing room, and he rolled across to the cold side as a well-trained travelling dog does. I turned back the covers. The bed was made up with linen sheets of a quality I had not expected here and a small bag of sea-lavender flowers was between them, smelling sweet and fresh. I was about to undress when I recalled the purse of small change that I had left by the fire. It is not fair to leave such temptation in the way of servants. I was not concerned for Kate, but the boy who had looked after Jonquil might come in early to make up the fire.

In my stockinged feet I crept along the passage and opened the door of the messing-room. Kate stood naked before the fire washing her body with a cloth, which she dipped in a clay bowl. The hot water pot that had been over the fire stood nearby. The gentlemanly thing to have done would have been to withdraw immediately but I watched as King David had watched from the rooftop whilst Bathsheba, his neighbour's wife, had washed herself. You will no doubt recall that story from the Holy Book.

I held the door a little open as I gazed and it might have been the draught from it or a sense of being observed that made her turn my way, her body outlined against the glow from the dying fire. Something I had long tried to forget stirred in me, as it must do within the salmon as they yearn for a mating-run up the river to its source. I stood still and was unseen, for it is movement that betrays a watcher. Even a wary stag on the hill fails to see a still figure, whereas the slightest movement will have him bounding away over the ridge and out of arrow-shot.

Kate turned back to the fire as I silently closed the door. The purse would have to wait the morning.

I returned to my room, undressed and put out my boots into the passageway for the boy to clean. Almost against my conscious will I left one boot lie with the toe holding the door ajar; the sign used in the Upper Lands by the traveller to signal that a night companion would be welcome. Would Kate recognise it and if she did, would she respond? My heart beat like that of a boy meeting his sweetheart in the rickyard for the first time though I called myself all sorts of fools as I climbed into the bed, warm from Wraith's body, and waited there breathlessly.

I had not long to ponder. The door opened and Mistress Kate came in carrying a candle. Wraith growled and I kicked with my leg to let him know his place now was on the rug.

'Can I be of further service, Sir,' she asked and I noted a tremor in her voice.

She was as adept at the bedsport as she seemed to be at all other things, though when we rested afterwards she buried her face in my shoulder and cried. It was not the crying of a woman who has lost a brooch or such-like trinket; it was the crying of a woman who has lost something much, much more. She asked me to call her 'Kate' again and again until at last the crying stopped and she was calm and came to me once more.

When I awoke, she had left the bed and I found my purse of small change on my pillow. I arose, dressed and went to the messing-hall where Kate had a mash of porridge on the fire. Her brown eye watched the oats bubble and plop as her blue eye greeted me warmly. I noted that the black cloth was no longer around her arm and I considered staying another day and lodging at the inn for a further night but there was little business for me in the village and tongues might wag if I stayed further without due cause. Besides, I wished to examine the site where a retired gentleman might build for himself a small manor from the timbers of a wrecked ship if the King would grant him a ship-breaking warrant. This survey could be done discreetly as I rode away in that direction.

I settled my bill, modest as it was, and bade my Kate farewell before returning to my room to be faced with a dilemma. Should I leave a present of cash for her? To have done so would have possibly implied the status of whore. Any other gift would have been appropriate yet I carried nothing suitable as I normally avoided such encounters as dangerous to one in my position. Even now I realised that my status had been compromised. An enemy might challenge my rating of the village as inadequate at one hundred marks and whisper in the King's ear that I had been induced to keep it low. Yet for sure one hundred marks was its tax-worth – without a manor. A hundred and fifty *with* such a building. I left no present and felt that one would not be sought nor expected.

As I mounted Jonquil and tossed a penny to the boy, I was deeply, massively tired of this Assessing business, with its constant travelling, and yearned for a home to retire to, perhaps one on a ridge behind a fishing village with a friendly inn and a woman I called Kate but who was known as 'Aunt" to most of the children, and as 'The Ferryman's Daughter' to those who *thought* they knew her well.

Other books by Michael Tod

Printed Books

The Dorset Squirrels
Includes
The Silver Tide
The Second Wave and
The Golden Flight.

Dolphinsong

God's Elephants

The Ferry Boat
Finding a credible God

A Curlew's Cry
Poetry

eBooks

The Silver Tide

The Second Wave

The Golden Flight.

Dolphinsong

God's Elephants

The Ferry Boat
Finding a credible God